ACCLAIM ~~STORIES~~

FROM ~~~~

T ~~~~

"Marcinko satisfies ~~~~ ~~~~ing
more about the team mem~~~~ ~~~~ally
on the part of fans with business, leade~~~~ ~~~~eam-
building interests—to know how he selects and maintains
a team."

—*Tulsa World* (OK)

"When a guy who could kill you with his bare hands writes a
book, how can you not love it? Pick this up or he'll find you."

—*Stuff*

**AND PRAISE FOR RICHARD MARCINKO
AND THE ROGUE WARRIOR® SERIES**

ROGUE WARRIOR: OPTION DELTA

"[A] classic crowd pleaser. . . . Great fun, more intelligent than
you may think. . . . Marcinko's Rogue Warrior yarns . . . are
the purest kind of thriller around, with action, pacing, and
hardware galore."

—*Booklist*

ROGUE WARRIOR: SEAL FORCE ALPHA

"Entertaining. . . . Marcinko and his team handle, with gusto,
both enemies without and traitors within, using their wits,
a staggering array of weapons, and an obvious appetite for
violence."

—*Kirkus Reviews*

"Authentic. . . . This action-filled novel is a genuine thriller,
one that keeps the reader in suspense throughout."

—*The Free Lance-Star* (Fredericksburg, VA)

ROGUE WARRIOR:
DESIGNATION GOLD

"Marcinko and Weisman add new plot ingredients and push them to the limits of military technology. . . . Half the fun is Marcinko's erudite commentary on the incompetence of U.S. military services, the complex and ultimately frustrating mechanics of international politics, and the manly art of protecting your ass."

—*Playboy*

"The salty soldier of fortune raises enough homicidal hell to get himself expelled from Russia. . . . Hard-hitting."

—*Kirkus Reviews*

ROGUE WARRIOR:
TASK FORCE BLUE

"Heart-pounding, white-knuckle, pure adrenaline action. . . . The fast-paced *Mission: Impossible*–style plot rockets along like a high-octane action movie. . . . A great book."

—*The Beaumont Enterprise* (TX)

"Extremely lively. . . . Not for the squeamish, politically correct or saintly. . . ."

—*Lincoln Journal-Star* (NE)

ROGUE WARRIOR:
GREEN TEAM

"Marcinko . . . and his hard-bitten Seal colleagues . . . come through, filling the memorably fast-paced yarn with vivid, hardware-laden detail."

—*Booklist*

"Liberally sprinkled with raw language and graphic descriptions of mayhem, *Rogue Warrior: Green Team* is the literary equivalent of professional wrestling."

—*Detroit Free Press*

ROGUE WARRIOR: RED CELL

"[A] bawdy action novel. . . . *Rogue Warrior: Red Cell* never stops to take a breath."

—*The New York Times Book Review*

"A chilling, blood and guts, no-nonsense look into clandestine military operations told like it should be told. It doesn't come more powerful than this."

—*Clive Cussler*

ROGUE WARRIOR

"For sheer readability, *Rogue Warrior* leaves Tom Clancy waxed and booby-trapped."

—*Robert Lipsyte, Los Angeles Times Book Review*

"Fascinating. . . . Marcinko . . . makes Arnold Schwarzenegger look like Little Lord Fauntleroy."

—*The New York Times Book Review*

"Blistering honesty. . . . Marcinko is one tough Navy commando."

—*San Francisco Chronicle*

"Marcinko was too loose a cannon for the U.S. Navy. . . . *Rogue Warrior* is not a book for the faint of heart."

—*People*

THE ROGUE WARRIOR'S STRATEGY FOR SUCCESS

"Picture Rambo in pinstripes. . . . Marcinko's style is inspirational; his (literal) war stories are entertaining; and sprinkled throughout are useful business insights."

—*Publishers Weekly*

LEADERSHIP SECRETS OF THE ROGUE WARRIOR

"Look out, Bill Gates."

—*USA Today*

The Rogue Warrior® series by Richard Marcinko and John Weisman

Rogue Warrior
Rogue Warrior: Red Cell
Rogue Warrior: Green Team
Rogue Warrior: Task Force Blue
Rogue Warrior: Designation Gold
Rogue Warrior: SEAL Force Alpha
Rogue Warrior: Option Delta
Rogue Warrior: Echo Platoon
Rogue Warrior: Detachment Bravo

Also by Richard Marcinko

Leadership Secrets of the Rogue Warrior
The Rogue Warrior's Strategy for Success
The Real Team

For information regarding special discounts for bulk purchases, please contact Simon & Schuster Special Sales at 1-800-456-6798 or business@simonandschuster.com

Richard Marcinko

Rogue Warrior®:
The
Real Team

POCKET BOOKS
New York   London   Toronto   Sydney

The sale of this book without its cover is unauthorized. If you purchased this book without a cover, you should be aware that it was reported to the publisher as "unsold and destroyed." Neither the author nor the publisher has received payment for the sale of this "stripped book."

Many of the Rogue Warrior's weapons courtesy of Heckler & Koch, Inc., International Training Division, Sterling, Virginia

 POCKET BOOKS, a division of Simon & Schuster, Inc. 1230 Avenue of the Americas, New York, NY 10020

Copyright © 1999 by Richard Marcinko

Originally published in hardcover in 1999 by Pocket Books

All rights reserved, including the right to reproduce this book or portions thereof in any form whatsoever. For information address Pocket Books, 1230 Avenue of the Americas, New York, NY 10020

ISBN: 0-671-02465-5

First Pocket Books paperback printing November 2000

10 9 8 7 6 5 4 3 2

POCKET and colophon are registered trademarks of Simon & Schuster, Inc.

ROGUE WARRIOR is a registered trademark of Richard Marcinko

Cover photo courtesy of the New York *Daily News*

Printed in the U.S.A.

This book is dedicated to our youngest and newest Warrior, Matthew ("gift from God") Loring ("son of a warrior") Marcinko. He wears that name with true spirit. He's been nothing but pleasure from the delivery room on, as he faces his daily challenges and subsequent accomplishments.

Contents

Rogue Warrior®:

The Real Team

u and I both kn

Introduction

Encourage and listen well to the words of your subordinates. It is well known that gold lies hidden underground.

—Nabeshima Naoshige (1538–1618)
in *Ideals of the Samurai*

I spent over thirty years in the Navy. They had me jumping out of planes and helicopters, scrambling up oil rigs and battleships, shooting-and-looting my way through many a hairy situation. They sent me to war zones and put me through firefights and, finally, they threw me in prison. You'd think that after I retired, I'd find a nice, quiet way to occupy my time. Golfing, maybe. Watching bowling on TV.

Fat fucking chance. Since 1992, when *Rogue Warrior* was published, I've seen more airports than a Jarhead has crabs. My dweeb editor refers to these cross-country barnstormers as my "annual book tour." Easy for him to say. Visiting more than eighty cities a year is more like the Bataan Death March. But what the hell—I *am* the Rogue Warrior, and you and I both know that if it hurts, I must be doing something right. And at least I'm no longer strapped to the cargo net on some "trash hauler"; they fly me on commercial airlines these days. And you can bet that a bottle of Bombay Sapphire gin is always close at hand. Many of you dedicated fans make sure of that.

You dedicated fans also have a couple of requests of your own. (No such thing as a free lunch, or a free drink.) You've asked me for more information about the Team members described in the *Rogue Warrior* autobiography and the six Rogue Warrior novels. You want to know more about these colorful guys—their characteristics, their backgrounds, what *they* think about our missions. The second request? Fans with business, leadership, and team-building interests ask me, "How do you pick a team?" and "How do you maintain a team?" Here, in *Rogue Warrior: The Real Team,* I'll try to honor both your requests.

When I was putting together the autobiography, the novels, and the previous business books, I realized there was no way to expand on the true character of the men who made it all possible. There was just too much ground to cover. Nobody (not even the most fanatical fan) would have the patience to read through an extra two hundred pages describing the colorful and deep-rooted talents of the merry band of marauders who've shared so much with me. But those men certainly earned the recognition they're getting here. Once you've finished reading *Rogue Warrior: The Real Team,* you'll see how we—and I do mean *we*—managed to succeed in so many missions that no one expected us to pull off.

Some of you want to know more about how I selected and maintained the team. You'll hear about that from my perspective, but you'll hear about it mostly from the men's perspectives. After all, nobody gives a rat's ass what a leader is *trying* to do. If he doesn't communicate with his men, motivate them, convince them to work toward the team's goals, all his good intentions ain't worth shit. You'll hear, from the men themselves, why they were willing to do what they did. This should give you the insight you'll need to use my priorities and techniques to build and maintain your own group of aggressive problem solvers.

Ten for the Men

You Rogue Warrior fans first got acquainted with my words of wisdom through "The Rogue Warrior's Ten Commandments of SpecWar."* These ten rules are listed, and illustrated in action, in each of the Rogue Warrior novels. Here they are:

- I am the War Lord and the wrathful God of Combat and I will always lead you from the front, not the rear.

- I will treat you all alike—just like shit.

---

*Created by Richard Marcinko and John Weisman, and seen in *Rogue Warrior: Red Cell; Rogue Warrior: Green Team; Rogue Warrior: Task Force Blue; Rogue Warrior: Designation Gold; Rogue Warrior: SEAL Force Alpha;* and *Rogue Warrior: Option Delta,* by Richard Marcinko and John Weisman.

- Thou shalt do nothing I will not do first, and thus will you be created Warriors in My deadly image.

- I shall punish thy bodies because the more thou sweatest in training, the less thou bleedest in combat.

- Indeed, if thou hurteth in thy efforts and thou suffer painful dings, then thou art Doing It Right.

- Thou hast not to like it—thou hast just to do it.

- Thou shalt Keep It Simple, Stupid.

- Thou shalt never assume.

- Verily, thou art not paid for thy methods, but for thy results, which meaneth thou shalt kill thine enemy by any means available before he killeth you.

- Thou shalt, in thy Warrior's Mind and Soul, always remember My ultimate and final Commandment: There Are No Rules—Thou Shalt Win at All Costs.

These were the rules I instilled in my men to guide their actions. I made these rules as much a part of our training as shooting or jumping or demolition, because they're just as critical to the mission's success.

But those rules aren't the whole story. I'd also developed rules to guide my own actions. More and more fans asked for guidelines to help them lead their troops in the business world, so I decided to write a nonfiction book to answer those requests.

Seven for the Leader

In *Leadership Secrets of the Rogue Warrior,* I shared my personal leadership code, the seven rules that kept me focused on the mission and my team through more ass-puckering situations than I care to count. Here they are:

- I will test my theories on myself first. I will be my own guinea pig.

- I will be totally committed to what I believe, and I will risk all that I have for these beliefs.

- I will back my subordinates all the way when they take reasonable risks to help me achieve my goals.

- I will not punish my people for making mistakes. I'll only punish them for not learning from their mistakes.

- I will not be afraid to take action, because I know that almost any action is better than inaction. And I know that sometimes not acting is the boldest action of all.

- I will always make it crystal clear where I stand and what I believe.

- I will always be easy to find: I will be at the center of the battle.

In *Leadership Secrets of the Rogue Warrior,* each chapter was dedicated to one of those commandments, giving both military and civilian examples of that commandment in action. Using these principles, you can prioritize your efforts for each day, each week, each month, each year. Of course, brilliant as they are, these seven principles don't give you a magic bullet. *You* have to get off your ass and function.

Fans responded to *Leadership Secrets* and asked for more. Specifically, they asked for guidance in dealing with today's highly competitive corporate culture. Well, I know a few things about competitive situations. So I wrote another nonfiction book.

Leading to Win

The Rogue Warrior's Strategy for Success: A Commando's Principles of Winning helps you punch through the chaotic, competitive business environment of today. Planning, training, and calculated risk taking—these play key roles here. As you move through these stages, you must have a strategic vision of what you hope to accomplish. You must be able to *see and feel* your ultimate goal.

How do you build that vision? You draw on your knowledge: the intel you've gathered on your company, your industry, your competitors, and your environment. You also rely on your dreams. That's right—your dreams. If you're working to achieve something personally important to you, you'll fuel yourself with passion and determination. But it all starts with a strategic plan—one that's thorough, realistic, and flexible. To help you come up with plans that'll win out on the corporate battlefield, I created the Rogue Warrior's Rules of Engagement:

- Aim before you shoot, because the "Fire, aim, ready" method is bullshit.

- Break the rules before they break you.

- Have character, but don't be a character.

- Lead from the front, where your troops can always see you.

- Don't confuse planning with training, or talking with kicking ass.

- Honor your boundary breakers as much as your boundary makers, because they're your point men.

- Don't be afraid to make mistakes, because the path to glory is littered with fuck-ups.

- Serve a greater cause than your own good, or you'll be a one-man army.

- Take risks—and more risks.

- Never be satisfied.

Well, the fans really took that last point to heart. You bastards just weren't satisfied with *two* books— you wanted more. Specifically, you wanted to know how to build and run a team. So here it is—*The Real Team.*

The Art of Teamwork

Remember *Star Trek?* The original TV series, the one with all the babes in short skirts? There's one episode where the pointy-eared guy is playing multidimensional chess—three boards, not one. Each move on each level rebounds on all the other levels, so every minute you have to keep track of a shitload of effects and countereffects. Well, that's what running a team is like. You've got to stay on top of a situation that's always in flux, where you're juggling a seabag full of men and matériel, and any one action has God-knows-how-many consequences.

That makes building and running a team more of an art than a science. It's hard to create a checklist here. What you do with your team draws on the ideas from *Leadership Secrets* and *Strategy for Success;* it's a cumulative process. So keep those first two checklists in mind as we move on to teamwork.

Building a Team

It's always easier to understand ideas when you've got a concrete example of those ideas in action. One of the most important things I ever did was put together SEAL Team SIX, so that seems like a natural example to use here. I consider SIX my military dissertation for my USN Ph.D. (which, in this case, does *not* stand for "Piled higher and Deeper"). SIX was something no one had ever done before—a "first" in almost every way. I wanted an organization that was operationally pure and stripped down, so I could get the most bang for the buck. To do that, I had to have the best operators with the support to help them perform at their peak. I designed SIX to be all teeth, and little or no tail, in contrast to the normal Teams (or any other organization), with too much tail and not enough teeth. SIX was as self-contained as I could make it. We all know how bureaucracy and organizational processes weigh down a unit, consuming efficiency and energy without advancing you toward your goal. I wanted to avoid that rolling snowball effect as much as possible.

With those goals in mind, here are the basic principles of team building that I drew on while putting together SIX:

It's the mission, stupid. You've got to define your mission before you do anything. This is abso-fucking-lutely critical. If you're not clear and precise in setting out what your team is supposed to accomplish, everything else will rapidly go to shit. Your strategic planning comes into play here. What's your battle plan? What are you trying to do? Are you assembling a kind of SWAT team to deal with a specific problem on a short-term basis? Or are you trying to put together a group that's going to operate in changing environments over the long haul? Each of these types of mission requires a different type of team.

A lot of the guys I selected for SIX were pretty green. Why? You might think that starting a high-pressure new unit, I'd look for mature personnel who've already proven themselves in the field—the top one percent. Well, that's a great approach if you're putting together a crisis team to deal with a specific short-term problem. But for the long haul, you need "cannon fodder"—raw recruits you can mold through experience and school in your ways. You need their youthful exuberance to give you new insights and a fresh perspective; you need the inexhaustible stamina of youth to make it all work, and keep working.

There's another problem with selecting one percenters for a long-haul job. Most organizations—in the military and in the private sector—limit the number of personnel who can rate that high. If you select all one percenters, ninety-nine percent are going to lose rank as soon as they join the group. So from their perspective, joining your team is a double-edged sword. Being selected for an elite group is great recognition, but their career advancement will probably suffer. That might be a sacrifice they're willing to make for the short term, but not for the long term.

Get your numbers straight. What's your budget? What's your schedule? Keep in mind that you'll never get as much time or money as you want. If you're given the opportunity, ask for the ideal—in Roguishly blunt language, if you're so inclined. (Hey, somebody higher up might screw up and actually give you more than you expect.) But from the very beginning think about ways to cut back. Identify the areas where you can cut corners without compromising the mission. Be prepared to sacrifice some options so you can get off the dime and become a functional unit ASAP. Either "build in" some niceties you can do without, or weigh carefully what you must have to be operational. Once you're off the runway—and demonstrating some success—you can start working on getting back what you gave up so you can sustain that success.

When I was putting together SIX, I knew we'd need all kinds of equipment—the best we could get our dirty paws on. I also knew it'd be hell getting enough money out of the pencil pushers and desk jockeys who okayed the budgets. So I needed men who could come up with creative ways of getting and spending, and I also needed men who could take what we had and cumshaw it, jury-rig it, just plain *make it work*. Putting those men in place gave me more flexibility when it came to budgeting. It even let me toss a bone at the bean counters every once in a while, just to let them think they'd won one.

This kind of strategic thinking is also a good example of the next principle of team-building.

Cover all the positions. Once you're clear on your mission, figure out what your team members need to bring to the table. No matter what your mission, you're going to need some people with technical skills, some people with communication skills, some people with organizational skills. Ideally, all of your people will be able to operate with some proficiency in all these areas. But everyone has a specialty. You want to make sure you balance out your specialists and get all your functions covered. That just makes sense. You wouldn't field a football team of eleven quarterbacks, would you? (Of course, we've all had head-up-the-ass bosses who probably *would*.) And speaking of football—one of my favorite quotes about teamwork comes from Knute Rockne, the legendary coach who, in the 1920s, put Notre Dame's Fighting Irish at the top of the sports pages all over the country. To this day, he's often quoted but seldom equaled. Knute always said about *his* teams, "I play not my eleven best, but my best eleven."

Running a Team

Once you've assembled your team, you still have to lead them. Again, look back at the principles in *Leadership Secrets* and *Strategy for Success*. They'll help you motivate and guide your team. The guys from SIX will tell their own stories about working on my team, but here are a few general principles that they all agree were effective.

Keep your hands off. If you've hired good people, you shouldn't have to keep an eagle eye on 'em. Good people, talented workers, resent that kind of baby-sitting bullshit. They want to excel and push themselves *because* they're talented. Try to supervise them too closely, and you'll destroy the initiative and work ethic that led you to hire them in the first place. Micromanaging leads to macrofuck-ups.

At SIX, I didn't breathe down the guys' necks, I didn't micromanage, I didn't tell them how to do their jobs. Hell, I didn't have *time* for that. I hired the best guys I could find, handed out assignments, and expected results. If I didn't get results, I found out why. I gave everybody a fair chance and made sure they had the resources and the information they needed. But if it turned out they couldn't perform up to our standards, I cut 'em loose. SIX was working flat out; each of us barely had time to wipe his own ass, much less tend to somebody else's.

Know your men—they're not machines. I'm not talking about those lame corporate get-togethers, where the peons are served some bad food and cheap drinks, and the man behind the curtain comes out to express his appreciation before he disappears for another year. If that's the best you can do, don't bother. Use the money to give everybody bonuses, or buy more sticky notes or better coffee for the office. No, what I'm talking about requires day-to-day commitment on your part.

Talk to your people one-on-one. Ask them how the job's going. Do they need anything to *help* them do their job? How's the family? These don't have to be long, drawn-out conversations; you're not trying to put together your own touchy-feely bullshit talk show. But you need to know who your folks are, what's important to them, and what problems they're facing, both at work and at home. These issues affect their perform- ance, which in turn affects the success of your mission.

Welcome mistakes. Mistakes are part of learning. If you're not making mistakes, you're not doing a god- damn thing. That's what's so wrongheaded about the Navy's zero-tolerance policy. Now, the same policy is infecting corporate America. Mistakes are important, and always will be. Not making the same mistake more than once is the key issue; you've got to learn from your fuck-ups. If someone on your team screws up, find out why. Did he understand his task? Was she running up against unexpected resistance from another department—or another team member? Fix the problems you can. Talk about what your team member should have done to deal with the situation. And *move on.* A mistake is not a problem unless the same mistake happens again.

Shut up and listen. No matter how smart you are, no matter how much experience you have, you don't know everything. You don't see every possible answer to a problem. You went to all this trouble to pick good people—listen to them. Let them give their point of view. No, that doesn't mean you have to act on what they say. Someone's got to be the boss, and that's you. But input from your people is valuable—let them know that. People support what they help create.

And if you do act on someone else's idea—do *not* pretend it's your brain wave. You'll just look like an asshole and piss off your whole team. They won't trust you, and they won't respect you. Give your guys the strokes they earn. There's no limit to what you can do if you don't care who gets the credit.

Share the wealth. If you're running a good team, you're pushing them hard, and they're working even harder. You have to keep in mind that these people aren't robots; they need little goodies every so often. Of course, everybody loves money, but you might not be able to hand out big fat checks. (And if you can, be sure you hand one to me.) Be creative. Say your team's been going balls-to-the-wall on a project for weeks. Look at the schedule and pick a Friday afternoon to send everybody home early. That doesn't cost much, and it'll make a big fucking difference in the way they feel about you and the mission.

Every so often, when I was running SIX, I'd "kidnap" the guys and haul everybody up to Whiteface Mountain in the Adirondacks, in upstate New York. We called it a "training mission," and we did get in some shooting and climbing and other op-related fun. But mainly, it was a way for the guys to blow off some steam after months of high-intensity, high-pressure work. You can't overstate what that means to your team. They know you see, and appreciate, what they're doing. And that makes them willing to do even more.

Eat the pain. Remember, loyalty is a two-way street. You can't expect your troops to go to bat for you and your mission if you haven't demonstrated that you're willing to go to bat for them. If they make a mistake, by all means get it corrected. Ream them out, in no uncertain terms. But as far as the outside world is concerned—and that includes *your* superiors—that's where it ends. After all, *you* hired the bastard; *you* trained him. If he screws up, it *is* your responsibility.

I promise you, there's going to be a time when you need an extra, even superhuman, effort from your people. You're going to need them to push *hard*—just because you ask them to. If you haven't already shown them loyalty and built up those relationships, you're shit out of luck.

Hands-On Training

So how does all this team building in the military apply in the business world? It's true that building teamwork is easier in the military than in the business world. In the military, the risks, challenges, and missions are more precise and well defined. And the stakes are higher; nothing motivates more effectively than the threat of imminent and bloody death.

But corporate teamwork can happen. It just takes more self-starting on the part of the leader—you have to develop the skills on your own and work harder to implement those skills.

There are a couple of ways to do that. You can read my nonfiction books, study the basics of my philosophy on leadership and team building, examine and analyze the examples. Apply those ideas, and you'll be way ahead of your competition. (Hey, I wouldn't take your money and sell you shit.) But we all know there's nothing like hands-on experience to make a lesson real. You just can't give somebody that three-dimensional, real-time experience in a book.

Corporate America is finally catching on to the value of the one thing the military does well—train leaders. There've been a lot of news articles about a new wave of military-style leadership training centers. Of course, most of these joints are put together by people who couldn't lead a horny sailor to a Saigon whorehouse. And most of them tend to concentrate on only *one* of the two aspects of training. They focus on gung-ho, Outward Bound–style physical training. Or they give their clients a lot of classroom seminars and three-ring binders. Neither one of these approaches by itself is going to be truly effective.

This means there's a wide-open area of opportunity I'm determined to exploit. I'll tell you more about that later.

Who the Hell Are *You?*

I'm not trying to be insulting here—at least, not any more insulting than usual. Before we get to the real-life stories from the team members, I want you to focus on *your* strengths and weaknesses, *your* working style. You can't lead anybody anywhere if you aren't willing to be as ruthlessly honest with yourself as with your guys.

I recently had lunch with a friend of mine, Doug Krug, and his son Matt. Like a lot of young 'uns, Matt is interested in SEAL life and challenges, and I was happy to fill him in. Doug and I also shot the shit about teamwork, corporate changes, and leadership in business. Doug, along with Ed Oakley, has written an outstanding book called *Enlightened Leadership*. With his permission, I'm borrowing his schema to help you evaluate your own style. (Hey, part of leadership is recognizing—and taking advantage of—other people's expertise.)

What Doug and Ed have done is create several checklists of extreme leadership and working styles—descriptions of styles at opposite ends of a continuum. What I want you to do is read these lists and ask yourself if the characteristics apply to you. Be honest, you lying weasels! What's the point of cheating on a test that can only help you? So even if it hurts your widdle feelings, answer truthfully. Think about the negative sections of your annual reviews, not just the positive ones. Think about problems you've had over and over with staff members, especially several different staff members at different times. No one else has to see your answers; it doesn't go on your permanent record.

Once you've answered these three questions honestly, you'll see where you fall on each continuum. You'll have identified specific areas where you can make significant improvements in your style. And knowing what's wrong is the first step of fixing it.

1. What's Your Orientation?

No, I'm not talking about your "sexual orientation." I don't give a good goddamn about that. I'm talking about your *thinking* orientation, the way you view the world. If you're a deer hunter, you've learned to focus on and look for the kind of movement that indicates a buck is within range. Same thing with the other parts of your life. In your work environment—and everywhere else—you tend to look for and respond to a particular kind of "game." Do you look for problems or solutions?

Problem Oriented

☐ Puts the spotlight on what's not working— what's wrong

☐ Looks for someone to blame

☐ Causes defensiveness

☐ Stifles creativity

☐ Causes more problems, as attention is drawn to the problems that already exist

☐ Drains off valuable energy

☐ Keeps us stuck in boxes

Solution Oriented

☐ Puts the spotlight on strengthening what's already working—what's right

☐ Develops openness and involvement

☐ Naturally moves the team toward the goal it's focused on

☐ Creates energy and enthusiasm

☐ Develops the atmosphere best suited for generating creative solutions

2. What Kind of Thinker Are You?

Okay, let's move on to your style of thinking. Thinking is the first step of acting—so how you think determines how you act.

Reactive Thinkers

☐ Resist change

☐ Assume they cannot do things

☐ Focus on finding problems to fix

☐ Become blinded by problems in a difficult situation

☐ Avoid taking on blame or responsibility

☐ Become limited by what worked in the past

- [ ] Lack good listening skills
- [ ] Run out of energy quickly
- [ ] Have a hard time choosing and deciding
- [ ] Feel a lack of control over situations/environments
- [ ] Often work extremely hard
- [ ] Fear risks or major challenges
- [ ] Suffer excessive personal stress
- [ ] Can't let go of the past
- [ ] Have low self-esteem
- [ ] Focus on what they want to avoid
- [ ] Do things right

Creative Thinkers

- [ ] Open to change
- [ ] "Can-do" oriented
- [ ] Build on successes and strengths
- [ ] Look for opportunities in any situation
- [ ] Take responsibility for actions and decisions
- [ ] Think in terms of new possibilities
- [ ] Listen well
- [ ] Have a continuous supply of energy
- [ ] Feel in control of their environment

☐ Can "work smart"—get results without working hard

☐ Energized by challenge and risk

☐ Oriented toward the present and the future

☐ Have high self-esteem

☐ Focus on desired results

☐ Do the right things

Remember, these are extremes of thinking styles. You probably won't match up perfectly to either of these descriptions. But if you take an honest look at your own ways of looking at the world, you'll see where you need to improve, the blind spots you need to be aware of.

3. What Kind of Leader Are You?

All right, here's where it all gets put together. Here's where we take a look at how you interact with and motivate your team. Remember—be honest!

Reactive Leader

☐ Needs to have all his or her own answers

☐ Is tell-oriented

☐ Makes all the decisions personally

☐ Pushes the organization for results

☐ Analyzes, analyzes, analyzes

- ☐ Creates sporadic motivation
- ☐ Is highly opinionated
- ☐ Teaches subordinates to expect direction
- ☐ Operates in a self-protection mode
- ☐ Fears losing control
- ☐ Focuses on finding and fixing problems
- ☐ Quick to fire those who fail

Creative Leader

- ☐ Has no ego-driven need to have all of his/her own answers
- ☐ Is listen-oriented
- ☐ Empowers people to make decisions
- ☐ Pulls the organization toward a vision
- ☐ Listens to intuition
- ☐ Generates lasting commitment
- ☐ Is open-minded
- ☐ Teaches importance of initiative and responsibility
- ☐ Models self-responsibility
- ☐ Knows that relaxing control yields results
- ☐ Focuses on building on strengths
- ☐ Teaches how to learn from mistakes

Remember, the point of all this isn't to make you feel like a worthless piece of shit. You're just trying to find out where your weak spots are, so you can strengthen them. No one's perfect, not even *moi*.

So who the hell are you? Now that you've taken a good hard look at yourself, we're ready to move on to SIX.

SEAL Team SIX

The challenges of commissioning and developing SEAL Team SIX were the biggest challenges I ever faced. Of course I'd want to draw on that experience to tell you about teamwork. When I was tasked with putting together SIX, I had an opportunity to design a purely functional unit, one without the now-normal overload of administrative tail. I wanted all teeth; what tail we had to have—well, we'd have to do it on the road.

The mission was defined—counterterrorism world-wide. The schedule and budget—now, and not enough. We had to be ready to move as soon as possible; mission planning for Iran was under way again. The equipment we'd need, the budget we'd need to pay for it, would be tailored as tasking and tactics developed.

That left one all-important element in my team building—*people*. I had to do better than the Jarheads; "a few good men" weren't going to cut it. I had to find the *best* guys out there.

The National Command Authority was seriously committed to the operation. The chief of Naval Operations authorized me to interview all Navy SEALs and any support personnel prior to their selection and subsequent orders to the Team. That basically meant I was handpicking my men. It didn't make me a lot of friends, but it did prove that there *is* a Santa Claus.

When you're putting together a team, you should always have a wish list—the qualities you're looking for in your team members. This is what I was looking for:

- Combat experience. Had a hated enemy zinged a bullet past his ear? Had he gone beyond training to the real deal? I wanted my men to be able to look in the mirror every morning and know that they could perform under fire.

- Language skills. We'd be working worldwide, among a range of people, both military and civilians. I wanted my men giving the orders directly, not relying on an "agent" or "interpreter." I didn't expect each man to be fluent in every possible language we might need, but I would need guys who could pick up enough to get by, and do it fast.

- Union skills. My men had to be able to rewire electrical systems, tap telephone lines, drive a truck through a "hostage barricade" situation. Sure, they were focusing on the primary mission—target acquisition or intelligence collection—but if anything broke down, they had to be able to fix it on-site.

- SEAL Team skills. I wanted SIX to be a self-contained unit, able to operate in any situation without relying on other SpecWar units. I had to have men with expertise in a range of areas: ordnance; submersible operations, such as diving; air operations, such as parachuting and flying fixed-wing craft and helicopters; communications and electronics; emergency medical care; and intelligence gathering and analysis.

- Teamwork. This was vital. We were going to be working so hard and so fast that we wouldn't have time to deal with personal bullshit. No prima donnas or loners. I needed men who'd proved they could pull their own weight, and more, on normal SEAL deployment. Sure, everyone has his own agenda. But I wanted men who put the Team's agenda over their own, men who could achieve their own goals without sacrificing the unit's effectiveness.

- Hunger. I wanted men who were hungry for action, hungry for achievement, hungry for challenges. They needed to be highly motivated, even aggressive. They'd have problems with routine, which was no problem for me because there wasn't nothing routine about SIX.

I knew that not every one of the men would bring every one of these skills to the team. That's okay. Part of the art of putting together a team is balancing the individual capabilities of your men with the overall capabilities you need to accomplish the mission.

Over sixty SEAL operators worked with me on SIX. For *The Real Team*, I asked nine of them to tell you about their experiences, in their own words. (The tenth guy was an "unofficial" member of SIX, but he was such an outstanding Warrior that I had to include him.) These aren't the ten "best" guys; every single one of those sixty men was outstanding. I could write five more books about each and every one of the men I worked with. But these ten guys were the real-life role models for some of the characters you've gotten to know in the Rogue Warrior novels. These guys all had something interesting to say, insights to share about their experiences before, during, and after SIX.

Now let's go meet the Real Team:

Larry Barrett,
    aka Bullet Head/Gold Dust Twin

Dan Capel,
    aka Nasty Nicky Grundle

Norm Carley,
    aka Prince Valiant, aka Paul Henley

Denny Chalker,
    aka Snake

Steve Hartman,
    aka Stevie Wonder

Harry Humphries,
    aka Harry the Hump

Mike Purdy,
    aka Duck Foot Dewey

Steven Seigel,
    aka Indian Jew

Dave Tash,
    aka Cyclops

Albert Tremblay,
    aka Doc Tremblay

Larry Barrett

aka
Bullet Head/Gold Dust Twin

Larry served with me when I had command of SEAL Team TWO; back then, he was a young E-4 petty officer, working in the Ordnance department. He's one of those tenacious bulldogs who doesn't let go when he has a job to do. ("Bulldog" is appropriate, since he had previous service with the Marine Corps.)

When I started the initial selection process for SIX, Larry was at the top of my list. Why did I single out this lower-than-whale-shit E-4? Because he worked hard at everything he did. The average person will put some effort into the things that come naturally and slack off on the things they're no good at. Someone above average will work at improving their weak spots, but they might not push as hard in the areas that come easy, relying on their natural abilities. The exceptional person will go balls-to-the-wall, no matter what he's working on. Larry was exceptional. "Diligence" is one way to put it; "can-do" spirit is another. He was always hungry to learn more, willing to go that extra step to become a more qualified operator.

(Just to clarify things—you'll hear a lot about both SIX and Red Cell, which are two related but distinct commands. SEAL Team SIX was charged with the mission of counterterrorism worldwide. That meant killing the terrorists or preventing them from doing their dirty deeds. Red Cell was designed to expose the Navy to terrorist tactics and help develop an antiterrorist environment throughout the Navy worldwide. That meant creating awareness and security pro-

grams that make it too hard for the nasties to get to you, so they'll give up and go down the street to the Air Farce base.)

There's another reason Larry impressed me. Most people's blood type is A, B, O, maybe AB; Larry's got something unique flowing through his veins—type L-O-Y-A-L-T-Y. He's not just loyal to me; he's loyal to his beliefs. There's nothing half-assed with Larry—it's all or nothing. *(You'll soon see that this is a common attribute among the Real Team personalities. There's no "gray area"—it's black or white. Compromise is not in their vocabulary.)* An example of Larry's loyalty: after I selected him, he made sure I'd consider his swim buddy from training, Frank Phillips. *(Frank is the other Gold Dust Twin.)* Not only did he make sure I'd interview Frank, he also coached him— told him to volunteer for the unit and not ask any dumb questions. Larry was loyal to his swim buddy, and to his new Team; he was a believer in the unit, even before the unit existed.

Another one of Larry's assets was his skill with foreign languages. He could develop a working knowledge of a language pretty damn fast; give him a few days, and he could understand and assess conversations and written material, and express himself pretty well—with one drawback. Whatever the language, he spoke it in a south Florida drawl. That limited his effectiveness in counterintelligence operations. No real problem there. We all have talents and limitations; the key is to maximize the former and limit the latter. I'd pick other guys in the Team for the verbal stuff.

But in every other way, Larry was terrific operationally. When he wants to, he can melt into the background and become wallpaper; he's got one of those faces that you feel like you know from somewhere. He mingles well with just about anybody; he can walk up to a total stranger and start a conversation without seeming pushy or threatening.

Behind that mild-mannered exterior, his brain is always going. He always has a purpose in mind; he's always collecting data, looking for ways to achieve the mission more effectively. He never stops learning, never stops passing on all he can.

Over the years, I had the privilege of watching Larry develop as a leader. He always led from the front and demanded top performance from his subordinates. He learned from the chiefs who raised him; he spent his time in the trenches with his troops, making sure they were well prepared, militarily and personally, for what they would face. He's a hell of an instructor—meticulous in his presentation, eager to explain the "whys" that make it all work. He never forgets that this shit was new to him once, too. I've also had the pleasure of watching him raise his two young boys with the same thoroughness and dedication. He's determined to pass on everything his father gave to him, plus whatever his "sea daddies" shared with him.

I don't want this to sound like some kind of "I love you—you love me" Valentine, so I've got to talk about Larry's flaws. His loyalty was so strong that his first impulse was to follow my orders or wishes, even if he saw a better way. He might not even tell me about that better way. He soon learned to speak up more often, and when he did speak, I listened. I knew his ideas were backed up with thought and merit. He never talked just to hear his own voice.

Larry was and is a "temple dog." Anyone would be blessed to have him in their organization. If the United

States ever needs his talents again, I know he'll be there in some shape or form.

Now listen to what a growling bulldog has to say about teamwork.

NAME:	**Larry Barrett**
DOB:	**December 22, 1951**
HOMETOWN:	**DeFuniak Springs, Florida**
MILITARY:	**United States Marine Corps; SEAL Team TWO; Mob SIX; SEAL Team SIX; Red Cell; SEAL Team FOUR, Navy liaison to the Air Force for SpecOps**
HIGHEST RANK:	**E-9, master chief**
SPECIALTY:	**Ordnance**
CURRENT:	**Owner/operator, RV park and nature camp**

First time I was in combat was Grenada. I thought it was . . . pretty interesting. We hit the radio station and received some fire, seized the radio station and basically stopped traffic. Not too long after that we started having guys arriving in these six-bys, armored trucks. That's when all hell broke loose. We had to shoot our way off the beach. Some of the guys had to swim out in the ocean and appropriate a fishing boat.

The first time, I guess, is always kind of strange. You're thinking, "Why are these guys shooting at me? I'm a pretty decent guy—why are they trying to kill *me*? Just because I invaded their country . . ." But it was pretty wild.

Combat can be terrifying, exhilarating, powerful—all these different things, depending on what's happening to you at the time and how well you deal with it all. And combat is relative to the piece of ground you're standing on. You can say, "Ah, Grenada wasn't much." Well, from my point of view, it was plenty. It all depends on what's happening on your little piece of ground.

• • •

My dad did a lot of different things. He was a ship-builder—built Liberty ships during World War II. He was one of thirteen children, and two of the boys served in the Army during the war. But he stayed at the shipyard. Then after the war, he did a lot of things. He trapped, sold hides, he opened a grocery store and filling station, he ran cattle—I think he had about 150 cattle at the most. He did whatever it took.

My mom pretty much ran that store. She did a whole lot of work herself. My father was probably the toughest man I ever met, but when it came down to it, my mother was tougher in the long run. She had to deal with me and my two sisters, and him. Strong woman.

My dad was a firm believer in work. There was no sitting around the house. Came summer, he found you a job, farmed you out to people around here, maybe clearing land with a machete or working for a carpenter. So I had a job every summer. Then, of course, we were always helping out around the store, pumping gas and so forth. This was back in the days of full service at no extra charge.

We had a unique childhood. That's a story right there in itself, growing up in the store. We had a pet bear, and my father brought home little alligators when he came back from hunting.

I always went to real small schools, so we didn't have a high school football team or baseball team. I did run a little bit of track. As far as classes go, I was a real good student, starting out. I was the secretary-treasurer of the Beta Club, an academic club, early on in high school. Then about eleventh grade, I started drinking and running around with the boys. My grades subsequently fell.

So by the time I graduated, I didn't have any real idea what I wanted to do. First thing, I got a job on a roller coaster, down in Panama City, Florida. This thing was advertised as "the world's fastest roller coaster." We used to get up there and grease the tracks every morning with axle grease, to make it go faster. Climb around underneath and tighten all the bolts that had fallen off the previous day. It was a seven-day-a-week job, from nine, ten in the morning to midnight or one o'clock at night.

I worked that most of the summer. Then I started getting bored. One day, I got on the ride, in the back car, and climbed out. You know those big springs that stick up in the back? Well, I rode those springs, holding on to the back end of the car. Rode that way all the way around.

I'd just gotten off and I saw the boss man running over. A few yards away, he slowed down, and when he got up to me, he said, "My wife saw somebody riding on the back of the car. I was coming over to tell you about it and then I realized it was you. You do that again, and I'm gonna have to fire you. How would that look in the papers—'Roller coaster operator killed while acting the fool'?"

Well, like I said, I was getting bored, and then a friend of mine got fired, and I got mad and quit. Then I got on a survey crew, clearing land for the Intracoastal Waterway. We cleared land through every single swamp for I don't know how many miles around. Well, that got pretty old. I knew these guys in the Marine Corps, and that seemed like a good deal to me.

I spent two years in the Corps, got out as a corporal. I might have reenlisted, but for this little problem I had. Once when I came home from leave I got in a fight with a sheriff's deputy. They filed felony charges and all that. When I went back to base, the sergeant said, "Look, re-up and I'll send you to Okinawa. They'll never touch you." But I said, "Nah, my dad's put up a whole bunch of money for my bond. I have to go to court." So when I got out, I went down to Mobile, Alabama, and then it never went to court. They ended up dropping the charges because the sheriff was basically harassing me.

Well, by that time, I didn't want to go back into the Marines. I started working construction, building high-rises, doing odd jobs. Just going nowhere. Back to my old habits—drinking, fighting.

I was hanging around with this guy whose dad used to be in the Navy. He was a plane captain on a carrier—the *Forrestal*. It caught on fire several times, so he always called it the *Forest Fire*. Anyway, he kept talking about the SEALs this, the SEALs that. It sounded pretty interesting, what he was saying, and I got tired of going nowhere. I told my girlfriend, who was about to become my wife, I asked her, "College or the Navy? Your choice." She goes, "Navy."

So I went down and signed up. I knew I had to change something, and that seemed like the way to do it.

• • •

I was in BUD/S class number ninety-two. I'm not really sure how many started. I believe it was the standard—about 120. We graduated about 20, with several rollbacks.

I don't think you're ever prepared for exactly what happens to you in training. I was thinking, "Well, it's gonna be tough, but Parris Island was tough and you got through that." Because I had prior service, I got to skip boot camp and go straight to BUD/S. So before I reported, I stayed around here at home, trying to get ready. I'm running and lifting weights five days a week, and then just blowing it all on the weekends, partying and all this.

I thought I was in decent shape. I got there about two days before class started and went running with some of the other guys there and I thought, "I'm gonna die. I really am."

But I knew in my mind and my heart that I wasn't going to quit. I'd make it or not make it, but I wasn't going to leave there because I gave up. They were going to have to kick me out. It was like working for my dad. This was my job, and I was there to get through it.

• • •

About Hell Week, the toughest thing I remember was the night rock landing. We were a winter class, we must have had twelve-foot waves at that point. We went out in the daytime, and I mean, it's rough. Guys are getting hurt, really hurt, thrown back against these rocks. When we mustered up for the night landing, I was thinking, "No way. It's all a bluff. This is way too dangerous. It's all a mind game." So we get the boats and finally make it out past the surf. Just getting out past these waves is tough. I'm thinking, still, "Nah, it's all a bluff. They're gonna call us back." But we just keep going, and I'm thinking, "They're cutting it awful close. They're gonna have to call us back pretty soon." And then I realize they really mean it. *That* was tough.

There was some helping each other out, then and all week long. But when you get right down to it, it's up to you. People can encourage you, but after a certain point, they've got to take care of themselves. They're not there to look after you. It's really up to you to get through it.

Back then, about all you had to do was *look* like you wanted to quit. Once you *said* it, you were out of there. Since then, they've decided, "Well, that's humiliating." It's not humiliating. I don't even remember those guys. All I remember is their helmet liners lying there. They usually rang out while you're going through another evolution, so you don't even miss them. You're just surviving. You're going on. You feel bad for these guys who didn't make it, but who *were* they? You can't remember who they were.

• • •

When I was in training, I called home this one time, and my mother said, "Well, how is it, son?" I said, "Well, Ma, it's pretty tough here. I'm just hanging on day to day." And I always remember what she said— she told me, "Well, son, if the other boys can do it, I'm sure you can, too." I'm thinking, "Thanks a lot, Mom. That's not any kind of advice." But it's really the best thing she could have said. *If they can do it, you can do it. Don't worry about it.*

I was thinking of that during those long swims in the Gulf off the coast of Louisiana, heading out to the oil rigs. If you judged the current wrong, you might be out there swimming for six or seven hours, and *then* you have to climb the rig. That would be pretty taxing. But you know—if they can do it, you can do it.

• • •

You know that old saying: Courage is not the absence of fear; it's the conquering of fear. There's always fear there; it's just a matter of overcoming it. I think a lot of it is peer pressure. Look at the Civil War. These men served with people from around home, and nobody wanted word to get back that they were a coward.

Just because you go through all this difficult training, that's no guarantee you're going to do well in combat. But if you don't do well in training, it's a pretty good bet you're not going to handle the real thing all that well.

These days, if a person wants to quit in training, they don't let him. They give him four or five counseling sessions, let him warm up till he's not cold anymore. "Oh, we don't want him to make a hasty decision." Well, in some situations, real-life situations, you *can't* quit. You can't just walk off. You quit, and somebody's got to take care of you.

• • •

Of course I'd heard all the stories about Dick—he was a wild man, he was a hard-fisted, hard-drinking kind of guy. Which was right up my alley back then.

The first time I actually met him was when we were unloading a truck at this place I probably better not mention. This was during the Iranian hostage situation, the buildup to the rescue. At that time, I was dipping Copenhagen, and I'd spit in this cup and set it on the bumper of the truck. Well, the cup turned over and spilled. I heard this voice, "Whose mess is this?" Plus a few more choice words. I looked up and saw Marcinko and I think, "Oh, man, I haven't even met the guy and I'm already in trouble."

When I went to work for Dick, I found out he was a great CO. The best I've ever worked for. Organizationally, he's probably a genius—the way he put SIX together, the way he utilized people in certain areas, the way the team itself was organized.

And he's an amazing leader. First off, he stood up for his men. And he was very personally involved. You felt like he knew what was going on in your life, he knew things about you—things that maybe you didn't even want him to know. He just kind of looked into you and really saw you, accepted some of your flaws and helped you use your assets. He motivated us to do things nobody really thought we could do.

I remember when we were getting SIX set up, he took the whole team out and got us free-fall qualified. I had probably thirty, forty static-line jumps at that point. But there's quite a bit of difference between a rope-a-dope, static-line jump, and free fall. Marcinko took the whole team down to Florida and we all got free-fall qualified—not just on parachutes but on the new square parachutes, which are very dangerous if you don't know what you're doing.

They laid us on the floor, and we all assumed these falling-frog positions. People would come around and correct you—"Ah, that knee's not right." We go through that a couple of times and Dick says, "Okay, here's the parachute." He shows us how to pack it. We pack it once, maybe twice, then we all get in the plane and go up ten thousand feet and jump out of an airplane.

I was scared to death. But it all went well. Everybody made it, everybody did the job, everybody learned. And that had to be done. We were behind schedule, and the Old Man told us, "Hey, we're going. There's gonna be no leave until we're all on line. We've got a mission coming up."

When you're in the Teams, you have to prove yourself every day. You can't ever say, "Yep, I'm a hotdog here, I'm just gonna lay back now."

• • •

I miss the guys more than anything. I don't miss the operations so much. I'm not going to go join a private skydiving club, I do very little diving, of course I'm not doing any demolition. But the other guys—they were my kind of people. We were a family.

Of course, families have conflict. We had conflict all the time. But that doesn't mean we weren't professionals. People called us cowboys, whatever, but we *were* professionals. We got the job done. We could go out with the Skipper and have drinks, be as close as father and son. But when the job came—duty came—the next day, then he was the boss and you were the employee. It just reinforced what my father taught me—do your job and do it well, and you'll succeed.

Marcinko and my father both taught me the value of hard work, of teamwork, of making sure your people were taken care of. I sure wish the two of them would've got a chance to meet. There are a lot of parallels between them. Maybe that's why I like Marcinko so much.

• • •

I left the Navy Halloween of 1994. I'd already set up a business, putting in docks and piers and seawalls, working with this Special Forces guy who'd just retired. We worked with another older fellow who had a barge, and he was supposed to sell us the barge, but in the end he didn't.

Well, putting these things in, it's pretty rough, particularly on your back. I got to the point I just couldn't do it anymore. I was going to see my chiropractor every day. So then I just kind of slid into what Marcinko was doing, did that for a while, worked with an old SEAL buddy, Chris Caracci, up in eastern Michigan, just doing all kinds of things. Worked with a buddy who's a captain on a millionaire's yacht, helped him bring the yacht down from Savannah to Fort Lauderdale. Worked in the air-conditioning business around here.

Then, not too long ago, I moved back here, where I grew up. Me and my sister are reopening the store, opening up an RV park. We've got to do something with the land—the taxes keep going up—so we're thinking we can put a nice RV park in, and keep it as natural as possible. We don't want to stack 'em in there like sardines. We want to leave some room, put some nature walks through there, that kind of thing. There's a creek that runs through the property, with very few people on it because we own both sides of it for about half a mile.

I wanted to come back here because this is where I grew up and it's special to me. And also, I have a nine-year-old boy and a three-year-old boy, and it's good for them. I'm trying to raise my sons the way I was raised—knowing the value of work.

This house sits on three and a half cleared acres, and part of it's infested with prickly pear cactus. You have to keep digging 'em up and throwing 'em away, or they keep increasing. So I have my boy take a bucket and go out and work on that. He'll work for a while and then leave. I'll go find him and say, "Look, I'm the boss, you're the employee. You cannot leave this job until you check out with me." So we're learning some things. I think his mother's going to have him washing

clothes, doing the dishes, and all that before too long.
Be good for him.

• • •

I definitely think there's a need for something that
teaches people how to work, how to think about
something besides themselves.

I had an old chief, Bob Shamberger, who used to tell
us, "Soft lands breed soft people." He always said he
was quoting Alexander the Great on that, but who
knows. I think we've come to that—we've become a
soft country. I'm a Christian now, have been for a couple of years, and I believe this country has turned
away from God and the Bible, the ethics and the
morals you need. And I think people are searching for
that. You get these executives going out in the woods,
beating on their chests around a campfire to act like
men—that's pretty sad.

• • •

SpecWar's become more and more pertinent to the
world situation. You can't always send cruise missiles
into drugstores and blow them up. So I think Spec-
War's going to be more and more utilized, and more
and more valuable. But I also think SpecWar has to
get back to the values they started with—hard training, focus on the mission. People aren't getting any
tougher, you know what I'm saying? People are getting softer. And if you keep easing off on the standards to accommodate the next generation, you're
going to have people who can't do anything. Let's not
deal with the quantity of people—let's deal with the
quality of people. You can take two thousand people

who aren't worth anything and you get nothing accomplished. But if you have two hundred of the right people, you'll get the job done.

That holds true for the Teams as well. They have to be careful they don't get so big that they lose sight of the goals and the abilities they had from the start. Now, you got all these admirals, all this structure. People need to just step back and look at what happened to Special Forces in the Army. They got more and more and more, and the officers became more and more in charge, and they created positions of higher rank, and people wanted to be there just so they could make the rank.

One of Marcinko's strengths was depending on the chiefs to run things. They've got their eye on the troops, they know what's going on. Most officers in the Teams—unless they're very lucky or very good— most officers never spend more than two years, maybe three, in an operational platoon. Then they roll into a training department, go out for postgraduate work, become XO and CO. But they never really are on the operational level again—not like the chiefs, who might spend most of their career in operations.

You can't have guys rolling through for two years, then becoming CO of a Team, making major decisions that affect not just his Team, but SpecWar as a whole. You've got to have somebody up there who knows what he's talking about, and somebody the four-star Army guy will respect. Not somebody who got there because of politics.

But that's the way this world seems to be. Things

get hot, and the pencil pushers run like rats, hide out—then when it's all over, they come right back and take over again.

• • •

We've all seen that happen. The suits, the desk jockeys, are in control when things are going well. Then, when the shit hits the ventilator, they abandon ship. That's the cue for the Real Team to enter stage left and kick ass.

Dan Capel
aka Nasty Nicky Grundle

$\mathbf{W}$hen I was putting together Red Cell, I knew Dan only by reputation—and his reputation made him stand out. Dan was one of those "young lions" who roars a lot and isn't afraid to piss off the older lions. He was just beginning to learn how to flex his muscles when the community started to practice a "zero tolerance" policy for expressive frogmen. I recognized one of my own faults in Dan. We both must have been on leave when they handed out patience. Dan has this energy level that keeps bubbling over; when he's not challenged to the maximum, he tends to ruffle feathers by just being himself.

Dan had already tasted combat; he could shave his own face and like it. It's a good feeling when you've been in combat and find out you can perform to your own expectations. Although he was still a youngster compared to the other Red Cell operators, his energy, youthful looks, and inquisitive mind made him an asset. It's hard to penetrate targets when you are—and look like—a 230-pound gorilla, but Dan could do it. He's such a gregarious, hey-buddy kind of guy that his adversaries never realize that he's a real threat to their existence. Doom-on-you time for them.

Why did all this make him an asset for Red Cell? Remember the world situation in the late 1980s, when I was putting together the team. The worldwide situation was changing. The United States was no longer worried about fighting the Soviet Bear in "over the horizon" warfare; new threats would be up close, dirty, and right in your face. Our mission—to prepare U.S. Naval installations and ships by conducting counterterrorist exercises around the world.

Dan's "fun and frolic" nature allowed him to get close to Naval personnel, both military and civilian. He could pick their brains, steal their ID cards, lift their installation passes. He was innovative in his approach and could tap-dance his way out of embarrassing situations. All that helped with the counterintelligence phase of the operations.

Here's another asset—even though he hadn't been in the Teams that long, he'd already picked up smatterings of foreign languages. (I'm pretty sure these skills were acquired via several "long-haired dictionaries" who could give him some real incentives to communicate clearly in the idiomatic native language.)

My biggest question with Dan was, "How do I keep him challenged?" Now, that's not a bad problem to have. I let him have the lead, developing contacts with other government agencies to broaden our technical skills and stay abreast of new devices under development. In exchange, we offered expertise to those who wanted to know more about shooting-and-looting.

Dan had no skills at the journeyman level, but he sure could break things, which gave him a lot of experience in good old reverse engineering. Why is this important? Well, if you're old enough to remember the World War II combat movies, the good guys always had guerrillas or partisans to "mule" the explosives, armaments, etc. In today's world those people don't exist. You've got to work with what's on your back. A six- or twelve-man team can't "mule" everything that might be useful. You have to be more selective, more flexible in what you use to take out your targets, get *yourself in and out. And once the conflict is over, it's often useful to get the target back on-line in the same speed. Reverse engineering has a lot of merit, and Dan mastered the technique.*

Dan is still an "idea" man—always looking for a better gadget, process, or business opportunity. Because of all of his positive attributes, Dan won't be satisfied until he's his own boss with unlimited horizons. He continues to grow in interest and talents. I know one day he'll stretch out and attack all the targets of opportunity within his capable reach.

NAME: **Thomas Daniel Capel**

DOB: **May 27, 1964**

HOMETOWN: **Pawtuxent River, Maryland**

MILITARY: **USN SEAL Team FOUR; Red Cell; USN Special Warfare Development Group**

HIGHEST RANK: **E-6, quartermaster**

SPECIALTY: **Ordnance and demolition**

CURRENT: **Training and firearms consultant, Heckler & Koch**

Teamwork saved my life. You hit a high-voltage pole, face first, going forty miles an hour, then free-fall seventy feet. You're gonna want people around who know what the hell they're doing, how to handle that situation, how to work as a unit to get you taken care of. It's your life you're talking about.

• • •

The whole nautical, maritime thing is the theme of my family. The Capel side of the family ran a ship in the Mystic seaport, up in Connecticut, called the *Australia*. Originally, they ran convicts from England to the penal colony in Australia. Then they came here to the United States and ran cargo up and down the Chesapeake Bay. At some point, the fine captain sold the ship for a bottle of wine. Well, there's some disagreement about whether it was an outright sale, or whether he lost the ship in a poker game. Either way, that must've been a damn good bottle of wine.

• • •

I call home Chestertown, which is on the eastern shore of Maryland, a little town established around the 1700s. The Capel family itself has a large clan on the eastern shore, and my mother's family is also from that area.

Of course, I didn't grow up in Chestertown. We moved around a lot when I was young—typical military family. Dad retired as a chief in the Navy—joined in the 1950s and essentially was your bell-bottom-wearing sailor. He was an aviation ordnanceman, so he did a lot of air time. We lived down in Florida, the Naval air stations there, then on to California. That's when he spent some time in the brown water Navy on PBRs in Vietnam. After that he went back onto sea duty, and he retired on the East Coast.

My father has four brothers, and all of them were in the Navy, too. Three of the five brothers are retired chiefs. One of my mother's brothers was a Marine, and of course all the Navy guys didn't give him any shit whatsoever. And then there was my grandfather on my mother's side who was also a chief in the Navy. He was a Seabee in World War II—part of the island-hopping campaign. So if you add up all the time my family's served in the Navy, it's way past the two-hundred-year mark.

• • •

When I was in the second grade, Mrs. Lubke passed out this little test, and one of the questions was, "What are you afraid of?" And I wrote in, "Gorillas and girls." The next question was, "What do you want to be when you grow up?" and I wrote down in big bold letters, "FROGMAN."

There was a book in the school library called *Frogmen and Parachutes.* Every single day, from the second grade to the fifth grade, I checked out that book. I thought being a frogman was the coolest thing in the world. Still do.

• • •

I always say the farthest I got in school was sixth grade. I figure after the sixth grade I pretty much cheated my way through. In high school I had a band of girls who'd do my homework for me just before the class. I wasn't scared of girls by then.

I'd think, "What the hell do I need trigonometry for?"—just like every other kid out there. So I focused a lot on sports, and of course extracurricular activities. Drinking in the parking lot, urinating on my friends' cars.

I played three sports—soccer, wrestling, and lacrosse. My senior year in high school I was offered eight full-ride scholarships for soccer, or lacrosse, or a combination of both. I played goalkeeper in soccer. I held the school record—twenty-seven saves in one game. We were obviously being stomped. In wrestling, I was the one who got stomped.

I decided when I was a teenager I wanted to be the first Naval officer in the Capel family. Growing up right there on the eastern shore, looking across the bay, all the guys from the Naval Academy running around in their white uniforms looked pretty cool to me. My senior year of high school, I received a congressional nomination and also a presidential nomination. Apparently the president gives out two nominations per state, and I received one of them based on nothing more than family history.

But I ended up not getting an appointment, for a number of different reasons. During my oral boards, my father—God bless him—basically told them to fuck off. The interviewers asked what he made, salary-wise. My father had just retired from the Navy, and we were actually doing farmwork to keep the bills paid. But because of a sense of pride and so forth, my father said, "My income is none of your business. That has nothing to do with my son's education."

They said, "Well, the alumni committee would like to know."

"It's none of the alumni committee's business."

They never did get that information.

There were some other factors, too; I'd been playing high school lacrosse, and I'd really ticked off the lacrosse coach at Navy. Things like that.

Basically, I received a letter from the Academy saying my SAT scores were too low. I believe you need a minimum of 1200, and I had 1150 or so. What I did was request all the SAT scores for all the football players, just to see what their scores were. I never got that information.

I'd put off all the athletic scholarships because I wanted the Naval Academy appointment, and I was giving that one hundred percent. So by the time they came back and said no, the other schools had moved on. It was kind of all-or-nothing toward the Naval Academy. When they sent me that letter, I said the hell with them. I was going to be a frogman anyway—I'll just join the Navy.

• • •

I was the honor recruit at boot camp. Top dog in my little boot camp class. Boot camp for me was nine weeks long, because they integrated A-school, which is your rating school, whereas before boot camp used to be thirteen or eighteen weeks long. Hell, when my dad went through, I think it was twenty-four weeks and they killed half the people and everyone had to walk in snow barefoot. That's what he says, anyway.

At some point, the company was sent over to the pool. There was a guy from the SEALs and a guy from EOD to motivate people to volunteer—like I needed any motivation—and they showed this film, *Men in Green Faces*. They throw on this 8mm film and I'm saying, "Now *that* is what I've been trying to do. Marching around in these little bell-bottom suits is not my deal. I want to do *that*."

So after the little film was over you could sign up for the screening test. That consisted of swimming five hundred yards, then push-ups and sit-ups and pull-ups, run a mile and a half in long pants and boots under a certain amount of time. So I signed up and I completed the screening test. They have different levels, all time related. If you want to go to BUD/S, you have to have better times. So I made the best times and I could have done either SEALs or EOD.

Another twist of fate—the SEAL motivator wasn't there the day I did my screening test. This has always been a point of contention with me. So the EOD motivator got me to sign up for EOD school.

Going through EOD school at the time were a few SEALs—Blair Oakes, Greg Philpott, Kurt Campbell. I developed quite a relationship with these frogmen. At that time, SEAL Team had the Mammal Program, where they trained and worked with porpoises and seals, real seals. It was being turned over to the EOD program because it fit their mission profile better. The guys that had been involved with the Mammal Program now had to go through EOD to continue with it.

So there I am in SCUBA school for EOD, having the time of my life. I have more energy than a two-year-old kid. I think I probably slept two hours the entire time. I was driving everybody insane. These SEALs see me running around like a maniac, and they say, "What are you doing here?"

"Hey, I'm learning this and I'm learning that. I'm having the time of my life."

"No, what are you *really* doing here? In EOD school? You don't belong here."

It started to dawn on me that I'd really love to blow something up. That'd be really cool. But disarming something that *may* blow up—that doesn't sound like good sense to me. Blow in place—that makes sense to me. I'm thinking, "Taj Mahal, fine. Blow in place."

"No, we can't do that. We gotta disarm."

Why? If there's no one standing there, why am I risking my life to disarm the damn thing? And even worse than that, I'm just standing there handing the wrench to the goofy guy who's supposed to disarm it. What kind of sense does that make? *[If you haven't picked it up from the context, what Dan means by "blow in place" is just that—explode that cockbreath right there. You don't try to disarm the weapon; you just put a charge on it, detonate it, and destroy it on-site. Sure, there's damage to the structure the weapon's attached to, but it's safer for the men—no risk of getting hurt while trying to make the charge safe. Just blow and go!]*

So when these guys asked me, "Dan, what are you doing here? You have too much energy for this. You'd be a great frogman, you'd be a great SEAL," I about screamed, "That's what I've been trying to do!"

So I did what I've done in making a lot of decisions in my life. I said, "Yeah, you're right. I'm going to go over and get transferred."

"Don't you want to think about it?"

"No."

So I went over and asked to drop out of EOD school—the only school I ever dropped out of in my entire life—to get orders to BUD/S.

I get orders to the very next class, in about three weeks. Of course by this time I've been exposed to the mystique of the SEAL Teams, and I'm sporting an extra tire around my waist—I'm wondering if I can really do this, wondering about the shape I'm supposed to be in and so on.

Two days after I get my orders, I twist my left ankle and tear almost all the tendons. They give me convalescent leave, all the way almost up to the point where I'm supposed to check into BUD/S. Now I'm really panicked. I'm thinking, "My God, I'm already starting behind the power curve. This just can't be." I'm talking to all these self-professed doctors and medical experts—"The cast has got to stay on, so you don't move your leg so it has time to heal." "No, you've got to take off the cast so you can strengthen the muscles you have left in your ankle so you can carry on."

The day I left, I got into the Chester River and soaked that plaster cast until it came off. Packed up my seabag and jumped in my truck and headed off to Coronado, California.

I got there on a Thursday, and training started on Monday. Of course, my ankle was nowhere near healed. I laced up my left boot so tight, by the end of the day the lace marks were bleeding. That was my splint. I blamed my slow running on the fact I was fat.

I was not about to wait for the next BUD/S class.

This was my shot, my opportunity. It didn't dawn on me that there was any other way. My class number is 132, and come hell or high water, I graduate with this class. And that's the only thing I thought about.

BUD/S barracks has three decks. First deck is for third phase, second deck is for second phase, and the third deck is for first phase. I don't know what the capacity of the third deck was supposed to be, but it was so damn overcrowded, there were guys hanging out the windows and off the balcony. In my room we had seven guys on two racks and three cots. Up until Hell Week, I slept on a cot.

We started out with 120 guys; 18 graduated at the end, with 16 from the original class and 2 rollbacks. When Hell Week started, we still had seven people in our room. When Hell Week was over, there were two of us. I remember one guy from down the way asked if he could come and live in the room with us. There'd been seven people in his room, and he was the only one left and he was lonely.

• • •

Right at the end of BUD/S, I got an interesting letter—my appointment to the Naval Academy. So now I'm set. I'm going to graduate BUD/S and then pick up my original plan of being a naval officer.

I asked to go see the CO—Two-Ribbon Tom. He's got this Georgia-preacher persona, big booming voice. "Congratulations, son, it's quite the honor. I'm from the Naval Academy myself, I'm gonna knock my ring all over the place, blah, blah, blah."

I said, "Well, after graduating the Naval Academy,

I look forward to going into the Teams and continuing my frogman path."

"No, no, no, won't happen that way."

"What do you mean?"

"You won't be graduating with your class—you'll be leaving a few days before graduation. And we're going to make you go through BUD/S again to get back into the Teams."

I'm thinking, "That's insane. You're telling an eighteen-year-old who's wanted to do this for his entire life, who's just persevered through all this—you're telling him he's going to have to go through all of it *again*. Are you insane? Or do you think I'm insane? I mean, you can kick me in the nuts once, but me standing there, letting you do it twice—it's not going to happen."

So I said, "I decline the orders."

Two-Ribbon Tom about swallows his tongue. "You can't do that!"

"No, I *can* do that. I decline the orders, I want my orders to SEAL Team."

At that point, I look across the room at the third-phase instructors, all enlisted men, and they're like, Hey, this guy's okay.

But Two-Ribbon Tom kept after me for days—"This is quite an opportunity you're passing up, son. Are you sure you want to do this?"

I said, "I've done it. I'm not going to the Naval Academy. They can kiss my ass, and so can you."

Those screwy orders—I don't know if Tom came up with that, whether it was a "policy change" or what. I never investigated it, and I don't really care. I closed that door and never looked back. The path I took was perfect.

• • •

After BUD/S, I reported to SEAL Team FOUR. On my wish list, I'd put all East Coast postings. I looked at where the teams went on the West Coast—the Philippines, and the Philippines, and then maybe the Philippines. And the East Coast covered Central and South America and Europe. In the early '80s, you could tell that there was a lot of political unrest down south, and political unrest equates to some kind of interdiction. The United States being the world's police force, God forbid we should let anyone fight their own wars. We gotta go in and take care of things.

I was lucky at SEAL Team FOUR. My guess was right about the political turmoil, so I was involved in some situations in Central and South America and the Caribbean. I received the Antiguan Medal of Honor; I actually received a Navy commendation medal with a V about the time I got my trident.

The thing was, this was where I wanted to be. If I was full of energy before I got to the Teams, I was really out of control now. When you graduate from BUD/S, you're thinking, "I'm bad to the bone." But it's nowhere near the intensity that's created by the Teams. You've got that super motivation and focus, and you're put together with all these other supermotivated individuals all focused on this one goal—it's phenomenal.

I was lucky enough to come into the Teams when there were Vietnam vets running the training department and involved in some of the platoons. Taking that Vietnam experience and applying it to Central and South America—that saved a lot of our lives. I remember taking that information in like a sponge. I wanted to know everything that guy knew, I wanted to be just like him, and at the same time, I wanted to be *better* than him.

That's what makes the Teams so wonderful. "Yeah, you know I love you, old man, but I'm gonna kick your ass."

•   •   •

This is my first combat experience. I was on the Rio Coco between Honduras and Nicaragua. We were doing sneak-and-peeks across the Nicaraguan border. This was when Libya was going nuts and Reagan was sending bombers over to kill Qaddafi and you had the whole Oliver North thing going on and so forth.

There were two targets we were concerned with. First, there was a DF site, a direction finding site, right on the point. The contras would have their radio transmissions, and this DF site could point them out and send their little Sandinistas over there and kill 'em. So we wanted to identify and take out the DF site. Second, there was an airstrip over there and they're trying to figure out what's going in and out on this airstrip, who's involved, numbers, all that.

We went in as advisers to show the contras how to recon these two targets. There were a number of support elements involved—riverboats and so on, some air assets. Under this shroud of super-double-secret mission, the larger the support element got, the more it seemed to hinder the actual mission. You had four individuals with all these people to support them, and what the platoon ended up doing was helping support the people who were supporting us.

Anyway, we went in, reconned our targets, ate bugs and all that stuff, and we were on our way out. I was a 60 gunner—I could handle the M-60 and all its ammunition, and still maneuver and work the jungle and be just as stealthy as someone really light. That made me a great commodity because I had all this firepower—I could suppress a huge field of fire and we could run away and I could be just as stealthy as a smaller guy.

So we hooked up with our contra counterparts and jumped in our boat, two rubber rating crafts. I was sitting across from the driver; of course, I wanted to drive myself. I want to do it all.

I remember coming out in the dawn, still that hazy blue thing. I remember putting my weapon across my lap and sitting there. The driver—he was with the contras—the driver was motorboating along, and I remember putting my face in the sun and really relaxing, finally breathing deep. The whole time you're on a mission, you're very aware of your breathing, and very noise disciplined, and we're just easing out of that.

Now it just so happened that as we're going home, there's a bunch of Sandinistas heading home, and our paths crossed. They saw us before we saw them. We essentially had our guard down. We were supposed to be out of Indian country, we're relaxing, we're on our way home. And what happened was, this little

Sandinista patrol set up a hasty ambush. The first thing I remember is this popping noise, this little firecracker pop winging past my head.

All this is happening in milliseconds, but it's all stretched out in my experience. The driver went to say something, and his face exploded. He'd been hit in the back of the head. Of course I wanted to make all kinds of jokes about it—"Was it something I said?"—but no time for that. He slumped down and I started to move, but then I just fell off the boat.

Of course wearing a 60 and ammunition, I went to the bottom at about Mach 2. All the popping and the noise of the outboard engine—the moment I went underwater it was dead silent. So there I am holding my breath, and I'm thinking, "I could ditch all my weapons and gear." But I decided to just walk out like a hippo.

When I popped back up to the surface, I saw what had happened. The Sandinistas were very smart, set up a very classic maneuver. They hit us at a crook or a corner of the river, where we had to slow down for that turn. I came out of the boat before it got to the corner, and they kept going, so I was off to the side of the line of fire. No one even realized I was over there.

The other SEALs were taking them on head-on, and they'd already started the firing movement. They were starting to gain better ground and move out of there. We were just on a reconnaissance mission, we didn't have a lot of ammunition—we just wanted to break contact, return enough fire to run away.

They weren't even looking at me; the Sandinistas

were concentrating on my element. I focused on my sights and took off the safety and squeezed the trigger. The 60's a shoulder-fired weapon, and I remember the bolt flying past my ear and hitting the chamber and nothing happening. I was sure they heard that noise. I'm standing waist deep in water, there's no cover or concealment. I dropped the gun down, reloaded the weapon, and came up shooting. What this did was set up an L-shaped ambush. The Sandinistas are caught between fire in front of them and off to their right side. Within the first couple of seconds, I'm laying down two hundred rounds of ammunition. I was cutting *trees* down. What this did was move them down to my unit so they could take them out.

After that was all done, we patched up the boats and headed back across the border. We lost the driver of my boat, but that was it. I don't think anyone else even got dinged.

I wish I could say that I planned the whole thing, but rolling off the boat was a complete mistake. And then I had to just make the best of it. That was due completely to the lessons learned from the Vietnam vet SEALs. These guys were just absolute legends. Truly the consummate unconventional warriors. Their lives were unconventional, their thought processes were unconventional. And that gives you an edge. You're drawing from all your experiences, things you did as a kid running around. Whatever works. You *are* going to reach that goal.

And that brings up training. Of course you've got to train, and train, and then train some more. Like the

Old Man says, "The more you sweat in training, the less you bleed in combat."

But what you don't want to do is shut down and go into this muscle memory thing or whatever they talk about. All that training is what frees up your brain, lets you take advantage of that unconventional thinking. You don't want to rely on training—you want to rely on yourself. The clearer head you have in conflict, the more successful you'll be because you can think of other ways to handle a situation. You can draw on all kinds of different sources. "I remember when I was a kid and I stuffed that firecracker in the wasps' nest, we could do the same kind of thing here, create a diversion." You're not bogged down.

But back to the Rio Coco. Eventually we went back in, went back to the DF site, called in close air support with a combat 130. They went in and destroyed the DF site, and we cleared it to make sure nobody was left. So the site was taken down, and the contras got their information on who came in and out of that airstrip. Missions were complete, and I'd had a taste of what the job was all about. From that point on it escalated, in the sense that I'm trying to get my fingers in more stuff. I became the adrenaline junky, I had to find out what was going on out there, who was involved, and this leads to my introduction to Dick and his organization.

• • •

On the Teams I'd strived to be the fastest, strongest, loudest, drinkingest, bestest. What happened was I came across people who were even more arrogant than me and I was ready to take 'em. Of course they scared the living shit out of me. These were the long-haired go-fast guys across the street at SEAL Team SHH. I was in SEAL Team FOUR, and I'd met a number of guys from SEAL Team SHH, and then I got to interact with a number of their training cadre, and then a number of their assault team guys. *[What's "SEAL Team SHH," you're asking? Well, that's more of Dan's humor. He means SEAL Team SIX, but he's making fun of the secrecy we operated under.]*

I don't remember the very first time I met Dick, but every time I was in his presence I was in awe. He was The Man. If you give me a few adult beverages and he's around, I think I embarrass him because I think so much of him.

I remember Dick during his hell-raising days, he was just about to create Red Cell. This is 1984, '85—I'm still a FNG in the Teams. Talking with the guys and getting introduced to Dick, which I understand now was quite the honor. I kept my distance because I figured, you know, people are so full of bullshit, and actions speak louder than words. Next thing you know I was invited to come up and screen and interview for SEAL Team SHH. Next thing you know I was getting orders to Red Cell, which I was clueless about.

At first I was overwhelmingly intimidated. I'd spent two years in SEAL Team FOUR and I was a big fish in a little pond, and then I was right back to being a little fish in a great big pond. The very first day was just like my very first day of reporting on to SEAL

Team FOUR. It's not that you're afraid, it's how you handle it. I just got in there and started mixing it up.

● ● ●

I said earlier that teamwork saved my life. Here's the story on that.

We were on a HAHO—high altitude, high opening—jump. It was a training venture, out in the Arizona desert, middle of the night. I had met Laura, who's now my fiancée, and I was enjoying her company, and the guys called and said, "Hey, where are you? We're ready to go." I want you to know that's the only time I've ever been late for a mission.

I was crew chief, and I always called the guys together for a little inspirational message before we went up. So that night, I said, "I just had the best sex of my life, and like Geronimo said, 'Today is a good day to die.'" The guys were all looking at me like, "What the hell's he talking about?" That's just what came into my head, honest to God.

Everything starts out great. We're going up with a bunch of guys from other branches, Army and so forth, and I get everybody into position and out the door. Looks like a beautiful stack, really tight. So far, so good.

Then, over my radio, I hear, "There's a guy about a thousand feet back." I don't know if he's one of ours or what, but I know I can't leave him behind. I pulled back to see what I could do. What this did was put us so far short of our target. I radioed to let them know I'm now going to take lead. We were going to fall six miles short and we're going to have to run this across the desert.

Don't take any of your gear, just grab your gun. Rizzo is our slowest runner—"Rizzo, you're going to lead us across the desert as fast as you can." *[Let me spell it out, in case anyone's confused. By holding back with the jumper one thousand feet behind, the rest of the team would land six miles short of the drop zone, or target. Instead of riding the parachutes all the way, they'd have to run across that six miles of desert to make it to the original DZ. If they held back any more, they'd be even farther from the target. The best Dan could do was put his slowest man on point to lead the charge across the desert, and hope the trail man would eventually catch up with the rest of the team.]*

So once I radioed everyone, I just let this guy behind us drift into oblivion; there's nothing I can do to help him. He was an Army guy; he'd forgotten to tell anyone this was his first night HAHO and this was his first night HAHO with equipment in a full-scale exercise. When he left the aircraft he forgot to count, and after that, God only knows what happened. He remembered to open his parachute, he got that far.

Then the moon starts to rise and it's really beautiful. I'm looking behind me, to make sure the stack's tight, and this is what I remember. I come around and make the final turn, and the moon's lighting up the chutes, and I think, "Wow, this would make a really cool scene in a movie. We're gonna land sixteen guys in the end zone of a football field. We're gonna be able to drop our crap and get going and we're gonna pull this off."

As I turn back around and face forward, there's high

tension wires in front of me. So I grab my brakes and I sink them past my butt. What this does is stall my chute out, and the wires whip across my ass. It felt like being smacked across the ass with a broomstick. I let the handles of my parachute go and put my hand on my mike to warn everyone to turn.

Now, after a stall on this chute, when you let the brakes go, that surges it forward, up to maybe forty miles an hour. But that's okay—I just finished looking down at my altimeter, so I know I have at least one hundred feet before I hit the ground. Things aren't looking so bad. Everybody'll still land really tight, and I'll land thirty or forty yards ahead of them. I have to give the guys the direction, and I'm reaching for my mike and looking back to make sure I give 'em the right direction, and as I look back at the wires, I whisper under my breath, "Hah, missed me, motherfucker." Then I turn around and face forward and key the mike. At this point, I'm doing anywhere from twenty to forty miles an hour. That's when I hit the tower and the second set of wires.

That hurt. I mean, it stung quite a bit.

It's all a little hazy to me here, but I remember the parachute draped across the wires, melting across them. I knew if I cut away from the chute, that's a hundred-foot fall—no time for my reserve to deploy. So I'll pull the chute off the wires and it'll reinflate before I hit the ground. Well, not quite. My chute—the part that wasn't on fire—never redeployed. From my boot marks on the tower to the ground was seventy feet. I took it, basically, in free fall.

I was the lowest man in the stack, so the guys just cruised right over the wires, they all landed in a little tiny circle. It's the middle of the night—two, three o'clock in the morning—so they didn't see what had just happened. But they missed my manic, two-year-old's energy, and they were all saying "Where's Dan?" Not in a panic, but "Where is that motherfucker?" We had landed so short that we'd landed in a herd of cows that were hanging around these high tension wires for some reason. And now that we've scared the shit out of these cows, they're making all this noise, "mmmm-moooooo," and there's me sitting on the ground calling for help, and nobody can hear me because my face is crushed and I sound like one of the cows.

They got me into the Tucson medical center less than an hour after I hit the ground—close to a hundred miles, in less than an hour. The Army guy who screwed up the whole thing, he patched in his comms to Lifeflight. They got all the comms on line and got me out of there.

That's the infamous parachute story.

• • •

I think the biggest problem with the corporate world is that it's run by people who can't do what they say they can do. I haven't found a lot of smart bosses in the corporate world—people who can identify their support element, their midmanagers, and so forth, and bring them along, motivate them.

That's what Dick has done so well. He took a look at all these guys, saw their different strengths, their capabilities, and brought them out. He made it possible for all of us to do more than we ever thought *was* possible.

• • •

There's no way you can beat me. You're just not going to be able to keep me down. And I don't think people in the corporate world are used to that—people telling the truth, taking charge, just being out-right, blatantly honest.

There's that old saying, "Do right, fear no man." Yeah, I'll run into problems here and there, but you're not going to keep me down. I will always come out on top, and the reason is because of my experience in the Teams. I'm not intimidated by anybody. There's no reason to be.

I've been exposed to an organization and an individual that taught me you don't have to accept limitations. You can do much more than you think you can.

When I got the call about working for Henry Kissinger, I stood in the snow for almost an hour and a half in nothing but a pair of boxer shorts. And the guy never knew it. I had to be outside, because the babies were crying. I had to be able to talk to the guy without the kids screaming in the background. My daughter, Sydney, hadn't slept all night, and she was teething, so I'm holding her, trying to get her quiet, when the phone rang.

The guy on the other end said, "May I speak to Thomas Capel?"

First off, he called me Thomas, then he said my name wrong, "kuh-PELL," so I knew for a fact I'd never spoken to him before, had no idea who he was. So I said,

"Yeah, this is Thomas kuh-PELL," with the "asshole" kind of implied there.

He said, "Well, I'm the director of security for Dr. Henry Kissinger and I wondered if I could talk to you about accepting a position here."

I said, "Let me put you on hold for just a second." I handed the baby off to the then-wife and grabbed the phone and walked outside. We were in Aspen, Colorado, in the middle of winter, and I stood out there in the snow in my boxers and talked to him for over an hour. Got the job.

When I was a kid, I'd come home and my mother would see me and say, "Oh my God, you're bleeding, how did you get that cut?" and I'd honestly say, "Uh, I don't know." My father would always say this about me: "No sense, no feeling." But in a way, I think that's very accurate, because I'm just not paying attention to the pain.

So it's not like BUD/S, or the Teams, or Dick taught me that kind of focus. I think it's something you're born with. But all those influences definitely channeled that quality, developed it the right way, turned it into a tool I could use.

I've got two kids—Harry, who's six, and Sydney, who's four. I look at them, and I can tell that Sydney has that focus, that drive, and Harry doesn't, not in the same way. Harry is the greatest boy on earth, I love him to death. He's a wonderful child. He's very thoughtful and sensitive. And Harry is in constant negotiations. I think he's going to make one fantastic lawyer. He's always looking for the angle.

This is how Dick put it the other day, in his eloquent fashion. He said, "Shit flies at your kids and Harry swallows it and keeps it inside and it bothers him. But Sydney spits it right back out. And spits it with aim."

This is a story that shows you what I mean. One day, out in the yard, Harry pulled a snail out of his shell. Laura saw this and she said, "You know, Harry, when you do that you kill the snail." The look on his face was, "Oh my God, that poor snail, I didn't mean to do that." Well, Sydney hadn't been at all interested in snails, but she overhears this and starts searching for snails to kill. Sydney will be in the pond, shivering, with her lips blue, and you'll say, "Darling, this water's really cold," and she's like "Yeah, what's your point? Can I keep swimming?" She's definitely got my intensity.

I was talking before about my grandfather on my mother's side—the one who was in the Seabees in World War II, part of the island-hopping campaign. Well, when I was about nine or ten, I was climbing around in my grandfather's attic one day, and I found his old footlocker. I opened it up, and his uniforms were in there, his medals were in there, and this packet of VE mail between my grandfather and grandmother. And the pictures. Of course I asked my grandfather about it, and the stories just started flowing. My eyes must have been the size of golf balls. I thought, "That's cool stuff."

So I took my grandfather's uniforms and medals, and my father's uniforms and medals, and my uniforms and medals and put it all in a locker for my kids to discover. I used to think it'd be Harry who would carry forward the Capel family tradition—Naval service, SEAL Team and all—but I'm thinking it might not be right for him. Sydney might be one it's good for. And that's great.

Norm Carley

aka Prince Valiant,
aka Paul Henley

You might think Norm's handle came from the fact that he's a Naval Academy ring-knocker with a silver spoon up his ass. Actually, he earned it when SIX went to modified grooming style. In his stylish coif, Norm looked like one of the knights from King Arthur's Round Table. A big-city boy of Irish descent, he was pugnacious by nature. And, as one of the vertically challenged, he took a lot of ribbing. He always made me think of a leprechaun with a little twinkle in his blue eyes that told you he'd just raided the cookie jar, or was busy figuring out how to do it and get away with it.

Unlike a lot of Academy grads, Norm never became a pompous pus-nutted can't-cunt officer. He worked well with the troops, challenged them and motivated them to peak performance at all the operational levels required at SIX. This served two basic purposes: one, he got close to the troops, just like all XOs are supposed to; two, he proved that they could trust him to lead them into battle and out the other side.

His contact with the men was therapeutic for him, too. Norm was stuck living in my hip pocket. We worked on top of each other, forty-eight hours a day, fourteen days a week, as we developed the tactics, acquired the equipment we needed, and fought for spaces to house this wonderful group. He also had to watch me wrench the system in my own inimitable way—which was not his way. He was the best operational partner I could've asked for. (Speaking of *partners, Norm's wife, Marilyn, not only supported him, but went beyond the call of duty by helping with a lot of those administrative problems that come up when you're on the road three hundred days, or more, a year.)*

Although I jab at the Academy grads, I wanted Norm as my XO because he'd been to the Academy. Growing up in the Special Warfare community, I'd learned that we were developing a corps of ex-enlisted and reserve officers who had trouble getting the attention of the "real Navy." Spec-War wasn't getting the proper respect or visibility because we didn't have officers with traditional credibility. In the Navy, this comes from the Academy, and only the Academy. I learned this by watching Captain Wendy Webber, one of our reserve officers, who became our commodore and did a tremendous amount to further SpecWar and put us on the charts. Despite his accomplishments, Wendy failed to make admiral—not because he didn't have the qualifications, but because he was a reserve officer. Mustangs like me and reserves like Wendy may be good at getting the job done, but they can't get into the "secret circle" to forward their goals and commands. It's not fair, it's not right, but it's the way things work. If you're going to get anything done, you've got to face the facts.

I knew I could get the command off the ground and ready to go, but if it was going to survive, it needed someone at the helm with the credibility the service recognized. That man also had to earn the respect of the operational troops. Norm Carley, aka Prince Valiant, aka Paul Henley, could do both.

When I was forming SIX, Norm hadn't yet been in combat, but he brought a lot of other necessary skills with him.

He had language skills from an exchange with the German Kampfschwimmer Kompany; during that time, he'd developed a valuable network of allied shooter contacts across Europe. He started out on day one trying to hone counterterrorist skills at Mob SIX, so he knew where to go in systems development. At least, he knew what wasn't going to work, so we didn't waste our precious time. When you're working under a deadline, that's a real benefit. Being an Academy grad, he could both read and write, which made my job easier.

Living together out of a seabag, like we did, we got to know each other real well, and we could talk freely to each other. He'd suggest the proper/normal/acceptable way to get things done, and I'd let him know how I was really going to do it, so we'd be on schedule to get the team ready to operate. He'd sometimes shudder at my Roguish rudeness, but then he'd put on his armor and charge through the door with me.

Most of the professional scars Norm bears are more my doing than his. You know—"damned by association." He knew the chances he was taking by linking up with me, but he stayed by my side through thick and thin—and a lot of days I was pretty thick. We did it, and survived, somehow. I told Norm that when he took over as the CO, he could use his skills and styles to work harder on the methods. It's a damn shame he never got that opportunity.

This was my master plan: Norm gets a well-earned rest at Postgraduate School, spends some time with his family, and gets away from me for a while so he wouldn't get tarnished every time I screamed "FUCK YOU!" to somebody who was in my way. He'd have time to strategically plan the organiza-

tional and operational changes he'd make once he took over SIX. It would have been a natural transition, and it would have benefited the total command.

But that made too much sense. The Navy bureaucracy decided that SIX would become a BONUS command; the CO rank was raised to Captain (O-6), to match the rank of the commanders of the other Tier One forces. That was unnecessary bullshit. I ran SIX as an O-5, and felt no pressure from anybody. I considered myself a component commander, at least equal in voice and probably more aggressive and tenacious in action. Norm would have continued in that tradition. I'm shit-sure that Norm got fucked out of what he deserved because too many people wanted someone to pay for my abuse of the system. Norm could have given a lot of examples of my negatives, but he still remains a loyal friend.

Now that we're both in the corporate world, we still toss bones to each other when we can. At our annual SEAL reunions, we compare our grandchildren and hope they get a chance to enjoy life half as much as we have. After all, SEAL stands for Sleep, Eat, and Live it up!

NAME:	**Norm Carley**
DOB:	**September 1948**
HOMETOWN:	**Philadelphia, Pennsylvania**
MILITARY:	**U.S. Navy SEAL Team TWO; UDT 21; exchange duty with German SEALs; SEAL Team**

TWO; assistant course director, BUD/S; SEAL Team SIX; Navy Military Personnel Command (BuPers); Navy Special Development Unit; Precommissioning Unit, SEAL Team EIGHT; SEAL Team TWO; Naval Special Warfare Group TWO

HIGHEST RANK: O-5, Commander

SPECIALTY: Navy Special Warfare Officer; Naval subspecialties: intelligence, strategic planner for Europe and USSR

CURRENT: President, AMTI—defense contractor and corporate security consultant

Being part of the Teams—it really was everything I expected it to be. I wanted the challenge, I wanted the chance to do something physical, all that. Jumping, diving, shooting—all that was great. Rock climbing—that I could live without. If you're climbing out in Monument Valley and you're on sandstone and you reach out to get a grip and the rock comes off in your hand—I just didn't enjoy things like that.

But every day was a challenge, a different type of challenge. That's what made life in the Teams so good.

One day it was an operational challenge, the next day maybe a leadership challenge. Or maybe you have to get the system to support you, an administrative challenge. But it was all interesting, every day.

When I first said I was going to go into the community, everyone said I couldn't because it wasn't a "career-enhancing" decision. "You're from the Academy, you can't do that." I just said, "Well, then I'll have a fun five years and get out. I'd rather do that than stick around and do something I don't want to do." I always said as soon as it stopped being fun, it was time to get out. It was fun all the way to the end.

• • •

Remember the *Rocky* films? That was my neighborhood—Saint Ann's Parish. We were Irish Catholics, next to us were the Italians, the next neighborhood over was Polish. It really was a set of ghettos—definitely not slums. These were all pretty solid working-class neighborhoods. But ghettos in the sense of ethnic groups living together. And each group really ran its little neighborhood.

My dad worked on the shipping docks in Frankfort Arsenal. He was medically disqualified during World War II because he had a bleeding ulcer. But he and my mother both came from large families, so I had uncles from both sides in all the branches during the war. One of my father's brothers was a lieutenant commander in the Navy. My godfather, a cousin of my father's, was career military—in the Army Air Corps. He traveled all the time, but he came around a fair amount, visited and sent presents and so forth.

I spent a summer with him in Fort Campbell, Kentucky.

My uncles really didn't tell any stories about their service—hardly at all. The biggest exposure I had, other than vacation with my uncle, was seeing pictures of all of them in uniform. Everyone had that dress uniform picture. But no war stories.

● ● ●

I was a pretty good student. I went to Central High School, which has always been for the quote-unquote academically gifted. I don't know how I qualified for that, but I did.

Central was an all-boys school. Originally, I wanted to play football and basketball there, but I was a pretty small guy then. I realized that anyone under a certain height and weight—it just wasn't going to happen. So I ran cross-country, swam in the winter and ran track in the spring and summer. That was probably the best thing that could have happened, because all that running and swimming certainly got me in much better condition than football would have.

During the summers I worked at a Boy Scout camp, but not as a counselor. I worked with a crew of guys doing general maintenance—nonskilled, non-union labor. Fixing up the cabins, the latrines, whatever. Get out there and get it done.

I really enjoyed scouting. I stayed with it a long time, became an Eagle Scout, senior patrol of the regular scouts. I loved getting out of the city. Growing up in the middle of Philadelphia, you don't see many trees. And I actually learned some good skills in Scouts—good survival skills.

• • •

I knew if I was going to go to college, I'd have to get a scholarship of some type. I applied to the academies, applied for the Army ROTC scholarship, the Navy ROTC scholarship. I'd always had an interest in the Navy, I think mainly from the old frogman movies.

The Naval Academy really was my first choice. I was offered both Navy and Army ROTC scholarships, so I could have gone anywhere that had an ROTC program, full ride. But I got the appointment to Annapolis, and that's what I wanted to do.

My family had no political pull. I got into the Academy as what they called a "qualified alternate." I got picked up by the athletic department because I had twelve varsity letters, every season from ninth to twelfth grade. So I think I was recruited for track and swimming. Then when I got there, I boxed instead of doing any of that. Running cross-country after being run all day as a plebe wasn't my idea of fun. Growing up in Philly where I did, I was pretty good with my hands. So I figured I'd try to box. And I did pretty well at that. Plus, it allowed me to vent some frustrations.

Back then, the SEALs were still very secretive. I didn't even know they existed until I got to the Academy. I was interested in UDT—those frogman movies, you know—so when I was asking about the UDT program, that was when I learned about the SEALs. It sounded interesting, but I was also told SEALs wasn't a career program. I decided I probably wasn't going to do it. But then my class was one of the first ones that could go right into the Teams—they started doing that in the '70s. Three people were allowed to go into the training, and I was number four.

That's another one of those stories that works out all right in the end. I went through all the screening for BUD/S, and I was number three. So I figured that's it, I'm going to BUD/S. I get down to Service Selection Night and they tell me somebody two places behind me had taken the third spot. Now I was number four. This individual had not gone through the BUD/S screening process, but they gave him the slot anyway. I still to this day do not know why they did that.

So I asked for whatever assignment I could transfer out of the fastest. That turned out to be minesweepers. I had six weeks of mine warfare engineering, in Charleston, on temporary duty. At that time, the mine warfare fleet was in tremendous flux. They were in such bad condition the government was just giving them away to different countries, refitting them. So I spent six months at the Navy's first surface warfare school in Newport News, Virginia. Then after that, November of '70, I transferred over to BUD/S.

• • •

I actually started training in January of 1971, so our class number was 71-01. If you go by the old class numbering system, it was class 51 on the East Coast. We started with 136 trainees, and 35 finished.

Going through BUD/S on the East Coast in a January/February time frame—that was difficult. We had eight guys rolled out because of frostbite. Of those eight, three actually had to have surgery. Little different environment than they have out on the West Coast. We had guys dropping out on the last day of Hell Week, being medically dropped. These guys weren't going to leave, but they were told, "You can't continue. Your physical condition—you can't go on." Those guys had a great deal of will—they were *not* going to leave on their own.

I have to say, I was pretty well prepared. Oh, it's physically demanding, very much so. But some of the mental games—they just didn't have the same effect on me, having gone through plebe year. So for me, the mental games were nothing, but the physical games were significant. It truly is a test of motivation. At some point as you're going through it, you hit a plateau. You're almost in a trance. You just finish what you're doing. That's all you can think of, finish what you're doing.

• • •

Out of BUD/S, I reported to SEAL Team TWO. I was there two days.

While we were going through training, we were all expecting to get in a platoon and go to Vietnam. So two other officers and myself reported aboard SEAL Team TWO, and the captain said, "That's all very nice, but two days ago they stopped sending platoons from the East Coast to Vietnam. You can either stay here, or you can go to UDT and deploy." Actually, what he said was "You can stay here with your thumb up your ass, or you can get out of here." So it wasn't much of a decision.

From there I went to UDT 21, came back off that deployment, and was sent TAD—actually, it was Additional Duty—to the Navy parachute team, while I was a sub ops officer at UDT. *[FYI—TAD stands for "Temporary Additional Duty"—orders for a temporary deployment, not permanent change-of-command orders. Of course, if you're working for me, it means Traveling Around Drunk.]*

From there, I went to the Defense Language Institute —DLI—and transferred to the German *Kampfschwimmer Kompany*, their version of SEAL Team. I volunteered to be their first U.S. exchange officer. Remember, by now, this is a post-Vietnam time frame. There wasn't a lot going on. Working with the Germans was an opportunity to do something, and I did that for almost three years.

Before I went, I had no foreign language skills whatsoever. The Navy sent me to the Defense Language Institute for eight months, but then the immersion factor is what enhances your ability and really internalizes it. Now I dream in German sometimes.

The biggest difference between the *Kampfschwimmers* and the SEALs is the size of the unit. They've only got fifty active guys, total. By charter, they do not have an offensive role. In our terms, their mission would be stay-behind.

Their biggest strength was in the water—they were excellent in the water. They really didn't have the unconventional land warfare tactics that we deployed. That was the purpose of the exchange—I was trying to learn from them in the water environment, and they were going to learn from us in the land environment.

While I was there, they had just transitioned to a new underwater rebreather, the LAR5, and I got the first unit in the *Kompany*. The way it works there is, they issue you a piece of gear and it's yours. So I brought mine back to the States, and we bought it for SEAL Team SIX. SIX was the first team to have a full complement of LAR5s.

Because of their charter, the German SEALs just didn't have the requirement for nontraditional missions. Every military reflects its culture, and for the Germans, obviously the effects of World War II were still prevalent. They didn't have an offensive mission, so they didn't do the same things we did.

But I found that the people we worked with—the people in Special Ops units all over the world—these guys have the same mentality. They have the same sense of humor, the same sense of purpose. I couldn't categorize the personality that's drawn to Special Ops, but there definitely seems to be one. I've worked with the Brits, the Germans, French, Italians, Egyptians. All these guys, all over the world, have something in common in terms of personality.

I think that's why I always thought of the Teams as something like a family. Everyone sticks up for everyone else, watches their own, watches out for everyone else. A lot like brothers. I can harass my brother, but no one else better say anything. It wasn't just the guys themselves—the families supported each other when the guys were deployed. If a wife needed something done, there was always somebody to help out. There was always a network. To this day, I know I could call one of these guys and say, "I need some help," and they'd be there.

I hear a lot of things about the changing quality of the people on the Teams. "They're not as good as they once were, the training's gotten easier," all that good stuff. I'll tell you what—the young kids today are as highly motivated as anyone else. They're in better physical condition than they used to be. But the sense of urgency—it's just not there. I think that's a reflection of our society. Things are pretty soft right now, pretty easy.

But the young kids who have a desire for leadership, a desire to do something meaningful—they're out there. And those are really dedicated young guys, guys who're ready to go. I don't think the mind-set changes. It's just more difficult to find those guys to bring into the Teams.

• • •

I first met Dick, I believe it was in 1975, when I was en route to Germany from DLI. I was picking up instructional materials, and getting briefed about all the equipment and capabilities. Dick was at a club at Little Creek, and I was introduced to him during a sing-along, the night we reported.

Of course, I'd heard about him. Everybody had heard about Dick—the wild man, the renegade. Back in '75, that was his high-and-tight days—no beard, whitewalls, short hair. Our interface then was real brief—"Welcome aboard. We'll put you in ordnance, everybody will walk you through the systems we have there, you already know dive ops, right? You're only here for a couple of weeks, have a good time here, have a good time in Germany, kid."

Then after Germany, when I was back with SEAL Team TWO, I started working with Dick when we started Mob SIX, the predecessor of SEAL Team SIX, putting the capabilities together. It was an interesting arrangement. I was at the unit, trying to put this new capability together, C.D.R. Gormley was at CINCPAC Fleet as the point of contact, and Dick was at OPNAV as the point of contact. I had to relay my findings to these guys, and eventually Dick, in his OPNAV position, got a chance to affect the staffing and put the Team together.

I was the ops officer at TWO, and it was time for my XO billet. I wanted to stay at TWO and be the XO there. Well, unbeknownst to me, Dick had other arrangements. He had me sent out to the West Coast to the Naval Amphibious School–Coronado as the assistant course director for BUD/S. I was supposed to relieve the guy who was coming in to relieve Dick at OPNAV. And then six months later I get a call from Dick saying, "Hey, you want to be a real XO? Come out here and work with me." I guess that was his plan all along.

I was real happy we hadn't sold our house back east yet. He could have let me know what was going on.

• • •

From SIX I went to postgraduate school. I have a master's degree in national security affairs from the Navy Post-Graduate School in Monterey. That was my break after SIX. All along, my intentions were to come back to SIX. I was told that I would be relieving

Dick. Of course, things changed and that didn't happen. Dick can shed some light on those events.

So after Monterey I was sent to what's called Navy Military Personnel Command—BuPers. I think I hold the record for the shortest tour at BuPers without being fired. I was there for five months, and then got a call to do another job. I don't really want to go into the details about that.

From there, I went to Navy Special Development Unit, and then was assigned to the Precommissioning Unit at SEAL Team EIGHT. During that time, they sent me to the Persian Gulf, in charge of one of the mobile sea bases. Operation Praying Mantis.

I guess that was the first time I was in combat. Out on the barge, we had missiles shot at us. It's surprising how much you *don't* think about it. I just went through the drills, running around to the stations, ensuring we were doing things properly. I was too busy to think about the consequences.

Again, when we were in Panama, it was just "do what you're trained to do." If you're trained properly, it goes okay. During those moments, your focus is probably more intense, the degree of anxiety is more intense. But you're just too busy doing your job to worry about anything else.

After the Gulf, instead of commissioning SEAL Team EIGHT I went back to command SEAL Team TWO. Put my papers in right toward the end of my command tour, did a short TAD as a command at Special Warfare Group TWO while I was getting ready for retirement.

Like I said, I'd already decided to quit when it wasn't fun anymore. I realized that the jobs before me weren't going to be fun. I was at the end of my operational life, and after that it was staff duty all the way. There was only one position in the Navy that I really wanted, and that was going back to the command. That was at least six years away. Six years, and a lot of moving around. My boy was an athlete in high school then, and I'd promised him some stability, so if I went that route, I was going to be a geographical bachelor. I didn't think I wanted to take that deal.

So I retired in January of '91 and started up a company. We're a defense contractor and we handle commercial security. Commercially, we do physical security assessments, threat assessments, risk analysis. We evaluate security systems and personnel and provide training, and we do some crisis response.

This way, I get to continue on the operational side of things. I do miss occasionally doing fun things I don't have to pay for. Now, everything comes right out of my budget.

• • •

I learned more from Dick than from anyone I ever worked for. The lessons were positive *and* negative. I think one of the biggest mistakes anyone could make is to try to imitate Dick. He's one of a kind. Those who tried always got in trouble.

But Dick reinforced what I always thought was right—you take care of your people, they'll take care of you. You surround yourself with quality people, and you won't have a problem. He recruited good people, he gave 'em a job, he let 'em do it. There was no micro-management.

I had a pretty unusual perspective, working with Dick, one that I don't think anyone else has had. There were three different places I interfaced with him. First, when I was at TWO and he was at OPNAV, then when he was at SIX and had the command. Afterward, when I left BuPers headed for that other job, I spent about three months temporary duty at the OPNAV when he was putting together the Red Cell Naval Security coordination team. Each time, I got to see a different aspect of Dick. A lot of people have opinions about him, but not many of them have seen all the facets associated with him. There's Dick the staff officer, Dick the commander, and Dick the mover-and-shaker. And he's effective in each of those roles. It's impressive. That guy—I've never seen anyone motivate troops like that.

Up to this point, I've never seen team building done effectively in a large corporation. Then again, the cultural environment of corporate America really doesn't require the same kinds of things the military does. In the Teams, in the military generally, there's a dependency on each other, a life-and-death dependency. It's one thing to lose a job, it's another to get shot at.

But that doesn't mean there isn't a place for teamwork in business. There definitely is. All the motivational training, all of those teamwork buzzwords in the corporate world—that's an indication of what people want, what they're trying to do.

• • •

I have to say, with the world situation the way it is, my business is increasing. There's more uncertainty—changing roles, changing operational environments, ill-defined enemies. The threat, whatever it is, is less likely to be an organized threat. The certainty of dealing with the Soviet specter is gone. I think the requirements for Special Operations and Special Operations units are increasing. The defense budget on the whole is declining, but proportionately, Special Ops is holding its own. However, we're still talking about just 1.2, 1.4 percent of the defense budget that goes into Special Operations. It probably ought to be more.

There's always a need for a well-trained flexible force, people who can deal with changing environments, changing threats. I think that's the trademark of the Teams. They're the best trained, the best suited, to meet the changes that are taking place.

Denny Chalker

aka Snake

Denny was and still is one of those Adonis-looking guys—broad shoulders, good chest, small waist, and an ass so small he has to keep a hard-on to hold his pants up. He's a natural athlete who runs like a gazelle, climbs like a spider, and drinks like a fish. Through it all, he stays focused on all other SEAL functions.

Before he came to the Teams, he'd served one tour in the U.S. Army, which was his appreciation tour—"Been there, done that, ain't doin' it again." He appreciated the operational opportunities in the Teams a lot more than most. He was selected as one of the young lions to be challenged and tested—your basic "cannon fodder." I knew I could throw a lot of shit at Denny and he'd never know he was hurting; he was too focused on getting the job done!

Besides being a superb physical specimen, Denny was an excellent gunner. He had the strength to carry ungodly ammo loads, and the muscle to keep the rounds on target even though we used "hot" loads and a rapid rate of fire. Since he was such a natural, it was always hard to figure out what he did best or what operations he wasn't excited about. He had the "can-do" spirit I look for, and the results were always superlative. When the proverbial shit happened, it was a pleasure to stand back and watch him perform. He took pride in all he did, even tending to his personal operational gear. It was his kit, and he made sure it was ready to go at a moment's notice.

It was my pleasure to watch him mature, see him grow—

however you want to put it. In the early days of SIX, he was an operational sponge, eager to suck up all the new tricks of the trade. He had so much individual pride that he made sure he was always in the upper performance level of all the functional areas we trained and tested in. Denny was a self-starter who punished himself first, then punished himself again, when functioning with his team.

By the time he came to Red Cell, Denny was a proven operator, now engaged in tactical enhancement. No more basic standards. How can it be done better? How can we train for Mr. Murphy? What is the "worst case" scenario? He had all the physical challenges under his control; now he was attacking the strategic thought process of mission planning and training for those specific operations.

When Snake felt senior/experienced enough, he no longer hesitated to attempt to advise me on operational, training, and personnel matters. He felt he lived in the trenches, and he wanted me to weigh the perspectives from that level. Even if I didn't agree with him, he just gave me a wink, a thumbs-up, and a cheery "Gotcha, Skipper." And he made things happen. The level and depth of his counsel grew commensurate with his experience and fervor.

I said earlier that building SIX was my doctoral dissertation in the military. Serving as command master chief played the same role in Chalker's career. Like so many Team members, Denny felt that sense of fraternal obligation, that need to give back to the source that gave so much to each one of us. While all those tadpoles were experiencing the harshest physical and mental challenges of their young lives, Master Chief Dennis Chalker was a role model, a goal, and an ass-kicker. For those maggots, he was some-

where between God and the Devil, depending on the day's wrath.

Denny doesn't mention it here, but in the midst of this challenging job, he got his college degree. You can view that as a personal effort for a personal gain, but you'll fail to understand the true meaning of the Team. Chalker showed the young tadpoles and the senior instructors the amount of effort needed to advance in Special Warfare today, the commitment to push yourself so you're better prepared to perform. You can't rest on your laurels; you have to challenge life and attack all adversity.

A top-grade instructor has to be a good operator. But a good operator may not be a good instructor. Some people have communications problems, or they don't have the patience to accommodate the level of the students. Denny is a tremendous instructor. He truly and thoroughly enjoys imparting expertise to those who want it. I watched him and his team work on the set of the Sean Connery–Nicolas Cage movie The Rock. It was a real pleasure to watch Denny handle the Hollywood flim-flam-wham-bam-thank-you-ma'am, and still keep his troops focused and at the ready.

He now passes on his talents through the auspices of GSGI with another "brother," Harry Humphries. Even in the afterlife, we continue to follow the rules of the Teams as we march on and meet all of life's challenges in the corporate world. The players don't change—only the ball field!

NAME: **Dennis Chalker**

DOB: **July 28, 1954**

HOMETOWN: Mantua, Ohio

MILITARY: U.S. Army 82nd Airborne
                   Division; U.S. Navy SEAL
                   Team ONE; SEAL Team SIX;
                   Red Cell; Naval Special
                   Warfare Development
                   Group (NSWDG); Com-
                   mand Master Chief Naval
                   Special Warfare Center
                   (NSWC BUD/S)

HIGHEST RANK: E-9

SPECIALTY: Boatswain's mate;
                   Instructor Rating

CURRENT: Self-employed contractor;
                   director of operations for GSGI
                   Inc., security training and
                   consulting company. Tactical
                   instructor and curriculum
                   development

The first time I was ever fired on was in Grenada. I
went down there on the mission with Duke Leonard—
we were the ones that went down to Ambassador Scoon
and got him out. Boy, that was a fiasco.

I did Copenhagen then, and I had the biggest dip in
my mouth. We were flying over the island and the
green tracers were coming in—the helo started look-

ing like Swiss cheese, and we'd overloaded it with people because we had to.

So we're in the middle of this, we're taking fire, overloaded as hell, everybody huddled up. And I looked over at the Vietnam vets—they're all laughing at me. They said, "So how's it feel to be shot at?"

I said, "Well, if our six wouldn'ta lost his tray cover, it wouldn't be so bad, 'cause we'd at least be firin' back."

Once we hit the ground, it took me, oh, about a half hour to get that dip out, my mouth was so dry.

I'll be honest—I'm not going to say, "Yeah, I enjoyed that. It made me happy." No, it's nothing like that. We were doing what we were supposed to do, and it was definitely interesting. But it's more than that. I don't know how to explain it. You train and train and train, and you always want to see how that training is going to work in real life.

• • •

There were five kids in my family—I'm the second oldest, and the only boy. My dad did a little bit of everything, all over Ohio and that part of the country. He worked for a big farm as a truck driver, then worked on another farm, a dairy farm. After that, he started driving eighteen wheelers, then he managed a convenience store. The last thing he did before he retired was start driving a truck again. I say he retired, but then as soon as he did he bought a campground and managed that for a while. He ended up selling that, but now he's working at an auto parts store, just to keep busy. He can't stand to be doing nothing.

My mom was from that area, too. Her family came from Bohemia originally, which used to be a country, but it's part of the Czech Republic now. My mother grew up speaking Bohemian. She was raised by her grandmother, who'd come over from Bohemia, and that's all she could speak. She came over and had seven sons, and all seven served in World War II—six in the Navy and one in the Army.

I remember my great-grandmother real well, but I never really knew my grandfather—my mother's dad. I call him Henry the Eighth, because he was married about eight times.

I remember he came over to the house one time, half drunk, with this pup. He says he's going bear hunting in Kentucky. We ended up taking his shotgun out of his car and putting him on a plane to Arizona, to my mother's brother. We kept the dog.

He actually didn't remember getting on the plane. Just got to his seat and passed out, I guess. He gets off the plane and says, "Jesus Christ, is it hot. Where the hell am I?"

Obviously, he was not the most responsible dad. My mother was about five years old when her grandmother pulled the kids in and raised them. So like I said, I remember my great-grandmother pretty well, remember picking up a few words of Bohemian from her. That's about all the foreign language I learned. Well, when I was at SEAL Team SIX, I took what we call combat survival language, in Spanish. Real basic stuff—I'm not at Level Three or anything like that.

Once my parents got married, my mother worked, on

and off. For a while, she worked as a secretary for one of the judges in Ravenna. As the family got bigger, she became a housewife, and then about eight, nine years ago, she started working again, in the bank in town. She's working now, in fact.

We moved around a bit when I was young. We lived out in the sticks at first, and then the state bought us out because they were building a dam. We moved to my dad's hometown, then a couple of years later, we moved to Mantua. Mantua's got one red light. The town itself is two blocks long, and within those two blocks, you got seven bars. The town's grown a little since I lived there. I think they've got two red lights now.

I played sports in high school—baseball, football, a couple of years of wrestling. As far as grades . . . well, I'll be honest—up to eighth grade, I did pretty good. Then when I got into high school, I started fooling around a little more, having more fun than maybe I should have. I was sort of like the black sheep of the family. My sisters were always on the honor roll, and here's Denny Chalker nowhere near it. I even had to repeat a class my junior year—government, I think it was. I didn't get along too well with the teacher.

But even so, my dad said, "If we're gonna put somebody through college, it'll be Denny." I told my dad I didn't want that. I thought they should help my sisters out instead. I wasn't ready for college. They were more prepared than I was. I wanted to go see the world.

I always wanted to get out. I was always outside, always out in the woods. I had my own campsite. I'd

just get out and do my thing. Don't get me wrong—
I've got a tight family, and I think the world of them.
But I wanted to get away and see something different.

My dad was not happy with that. He'd been in the
Army, in Korea, about four, five years. Got out as a
staff sergeant right after my oldest sister was born. He
never talked about the Korean War. I used to see his
medals and his jacket when I'd go up in the attic, but
he never talked much about it.

Well, I was seventeen when I graduated from high
school. I didn't turn eighteen till July. I wanted to sign
up for the military my senior year, so I had to get my
parents' permission. And, like I said, my dad wasn't
too thrilled. He got a little upset about it. Just didn't
want me to have to go through that, I guess.

Well, it took me about four months to finally get
him to sign the papers. I actually joined two months
before I left school. And then once I graduated, I was
on my way.

I spent three and a half years in the Army. In 1974,
the Middle East crisis with Egypt and Israel, I was
over there sitting on a runway with the 82nd
Airborne. And then, right before I got out, I was over
in Turkey for a NATO problem.

So, I did get to see a little bit of the world, plus Fort
Bragg, and that was pretty much it for the Army.

At that point, my intention was to go in for a tour
and then get out and play college football. In high
school, I played weighing about 150, 160. I wanted to
put some weight on. When I came out of the Army I
was up to about 200. So, that was my goal. To go in,

get out, walk on at college, and try to play football.

Which I did, sort of. That first spring, I was training with the team, and there was this guy who'd been promised a scholarship. He ended up clipping me and I blew out my knee. Back then, they didn't have orthoscopic surgery, so they just took my ligaments out. That pretty much finished my college football career.

So then I moved to Colorado, thinking I'd go to school to be a game warden, but then they were all booked up. I decided, what the hell, I'll go back into the service for a while. When I was at jump school in the Army, I met some guys who were frogmen. I've always liked something with a challenge. If somebody told me, "You can't do this," I'd go, "Bullshit, it can be done, and I will do it." And those guys definitely gave me that feeling of a challenge.

● ● ●

When I signed up for BUD/S, they told me that only 25 out of 125 make it through. And like I said, that interested me, that challenge

My class number was 101. There was just about exactly 125 of us maggots that first day. We ended up graduating 17. We had a total of 20 or 25, but there were a few rollbacks from third phase and second. Of course, we lost a few that got rolled back, too.

I mean, it was the typical thing. Before Hell Week, the place was full of guys, and then after Hell Week, it was just empty. Later, seeing it as command master chief, it just sort of confirmed what I felt about Hell Week back then, while I was going through it. It's the closest you can get to putting an individual in a combat situation—that kind of pressure, that kind of stress. I'm talking about mental and physical stress. What they want to know is, how do you adapt? How do you work, as a team, under that pressure? How do you function with no sleep? I think you get four hours all week.

I felt this at the time, too—once I'd made it to Wednesday, I knew I was going to make it to the end. I thought, "You can do anything you want to me, but I'm not going anywhere." And I've seen that over and over—if you make it that far, you'll make it all the way. You'll get a little dingy, you'll get your ups and downs. But you'll make it.

But that first Sunday night, Monday and Tuesday, Tuesday night—those are the worst days because you're still pretty much aware of what's going on. You've really gotta dig down inside yourself and just hang in there.

Remember, I had to quit football because my knee blew out. And when I signed up for BUD/S, they told me, "Well, we're gonna be honest with you. Your knee's gonna give you problems, so don't be disappointed if you get knocked out because of that." And I said, "Well, do I get a chance?" and they go, "Yeah, sure." I said, "That's all I need." You know, the challenge.

I'll be honest, my knee never bothered me. My tibia did, after Hell Week. I had a big stress fracture. I walked around with flip-flops for about a week 'cause I had elephant feet from the cellulitis. It took me about three weeks to heal up from that. But my knee never really gave me any problems at all.

• • •

Right after BUD/S, I went straight to SEAL Team ONE. I didn't have to go to jump school, because I'd only been out of the Army for a year and a half. So, the day after I checked in, they threw me in the back of the plane, tied an IBS to me. Back then we had the old release with the CO_2, and it drops below you and you land in the water with your IBS all blown up and ready to go. *[Denny's talking about an inflatable rubber craft— "Inflatable Boat Small."]*

Well, the jump master we had wasn't too good on the spot. So they stick Denny, the new guy, with the IBS and throw me out of the plane in Coronado. Everybody else hit the water but I landed in the middle of a ball field. SEAL Team ONE and UDT 11 are playing a softball game, and then here I come with my inflated IBS. I never did live that down.

So, after SEAL Team ONE, I went into Kilo Platoon. That was my first deployment. And when I got back, they had a platoon called Echo Platoon, which was equivalent to Dick's Mob SIX, originally. I served on that team for a year, and then Dick came out and did the interviews for the next team, and I was selected.

The first time I remember seeing Dick was when I was in Kilo Platoon, and I went out to Harvey Point for a demolition course. I think Dick was commander then, or lieutenant commander—maybe even younger. But he had a beard and a crew cut, and I saw him down there at the mess hall. Some of the other guys pointed him out to me and said, "Yeah, that's the guy's in charge of Mob SIX. The other officers in the community get all pissed off at him." And after I got to know the Old Man, I could understand why.

So later, I went to SEAL Team SIX with Dick, and then when Dick formed Red Cell, I went up there to be in it with him. And after his little fiasco—boy, they were really hammering us. I did my two years there and then I went back to Dev Group. By 1994, I've made E-9 and I'm asked to come out to take over the command at BUD/S.

You don't refuse a major command like that. And to be honest, I also looked at it like this—I was giving something back to the community for all they'd done for me.

Now that I'm retired, I still run into the guys that went through BUD/S. It's amazing. I've put so many students through, there's no way I could remember all the names. But they know you. Boy, they sure remember you.

• • •

I played team sports all through high school—football, baseball. And that's definitely one level of teamwork. But the Teams—that's another level. It becomes a brotherhood, a bond that'll never be broken. Even the guys that died, they're always there. The guys you worked with, even though we all split off in different ways, you never forget about 'em. It's almost like having a big family of brothers.

One of the first things I did with each new class was explain the term BUD/S to them. I said, "BUD/S isn't just Basic Underwater Demolition and SEALs. All these guys, you're going to create bonds with them and they'll be your buddies—it's called BUD/S—and then that will grow into what we call the Teams. You guys are gonna be cold, you're gonna be miserable, and you're physically gonna need to get close to each other just to keep warm. And that's to help each of you survive that situation, and all the other situations." And that's where it starts.

• • •

Motivation's not that much of a problem for me— at least, not for the stuff that's a challenge. But when something's boring—well, first of all, it's like the Old Man says, "You don't have to like it, you just have to do it." And I try to turn things around, give myself some satisfaction at the end of it. Set a goal for myself.

I'll be honest with you, some of the basic training gets old and I've got to motivate myself for it. So, instead of losing enthusiasm with a class, I'll maybe switch the drills around a little. Say I had them on the range and we're practicing marksmanship, using both sides to shoot. I might say, "Hey, lay on your back and get up on your head and shoot." Or if I have a ladder, I'll have them go up the ladder and hang upside down. Just to give it a little variety. That motivates me a little more, keeps it more interesting for me, and it's good training for them. And training is what it's all about— training and motivation, and it starts from the very beginning.

In first phase, the first I thing I did was, I got an IBS, a K-pot, and a paddle. And I said to the class, "First of all, this is gonna be your life. That boat is gonna get you in and get you out. On your own time, you're gonna have to patch it, you're gonna have to take care of it, you're gonna have to make sure it's inflated and ready to go. Your paddle is not only a paddle, but it's your weapon. And if you lose that coming in, then you're useless, so you guard that with your life. Your K-pot—if you don't take care of that, check the straps, get 'em replaced when they need it, then it's gonna fail you, you're gonna fail, and you're gonna let the team down."

I'd also use situations from SEAL Team SIX, my own personal experiences in Grenada, Panama, Haiti, El Salvador. I related everything we did in training to real combat situations and kept them motivated that way.

And I just kept preaching the Team—you're not an individual here. I told them, "There is no *I* in Team. If you're an individual, you're gonna get weeded out. You're gonna learn, some of you are strong in some things, some are strong in other things. But the thing that makes a successful operation is working as a team. That's what'll get you through the problem. You've got to throw aside personality conflicts and all that, or things aren't gonna work."

It's not all that much different in business, you know? People say, "Yeah, we're all working together as a team but someone's name is gonna be on this report. Someone's gonna get credit for it." Well, it's like making rank in the military. Not everybody can get promoted, and nobody gets promoted by themselves. Yeah, I made it all the way up to E-9, but that wasn't me solely. It was all the different things that I was involved in, with all those other people.

The way I look at it is, if everybody's doing their job, everybody will get rewarded, one way or the other. It comes back to motivation. Maybe your payment isn't the promotion, it's that you learn a new skill that you can use in a new job.

• • •

Years ago, before the overthrow in Haiti, eight of us went in and got an eighteen-month-old baby out of the country, along with the family. The reason why I remember this so well is this was the smallest number of guys I worked with in a real-life situation—four guys and two boat crews. And there was never a shot fired.

We went across the beach, penetrated into the city, got the family members. Came back out and rendezvoused out at sea, just over the horizon. And off we went. Not one shot fired. But there were people, soldiers, all around the area. So it could've become a little bit hot. It took a lot of planning to make it all run right.

Then there was Panama. Totally different situation. I felt like LA SWAT, but it was fun. Just going in, doing our thing. Looking for intel, trying to find Noriega, kicking doors in, breaching, checking tunnels, etc. We had farmers with AKs bopping at guys when they're coming in. They were so far away, they weren't hitting anything, so it was fun.

You know, the missions we got, especially on SEAL Team SIX, those were the missions nobody else wanted. And we used to take 'em and make it work. Like I said, if somebody says it can't be done, I will prove that it can be done.

I'm ready to go right now. If they called me back and said, "Hey, Denny, we need you back in," I'd say, "Do I get to be number one man and kick the door in?"

• • •

Overcoming fear? I don't look at it as fear. I look at it as an adrenaline rush.

The first thing I do when I'm tasked with something is look at all the situations and the consequences, the possible outcomes of what you're about to do. And that really helps overcome fear—planning for these situations and having backups.

But think about jumping—if you lose the butterflies before you go out the door, then it's time to quit, because you lose the aspect of safety. I look at fear, being scared, the same way. I'm not so afraid that it keeps me from doing anything, but I'm also not going to just run out and do it. I mean, we *are* going to do it, but we're going to weigh the measures. We'll have a priority way of doing it, a backup, and then another backup. And that's not the same as overplanning. Everybody talks about "what ifs." I don't believe in "what ifs." You keep it simple, anything's gonna work.

• • •

Dick's one of the few officers I'd follow anywhere, anytime. The support he brought to the Teams, his attitude—it wasn't like most officers. They sit there and say, "This is the only way we're gonna do it—my way." Dick was very open. He trusted his enlisted guys. He tasked us with things.

I remember handling all the communications. He'd say, "Denny, what do we need?"

"This is what we need, Skipper."

"Okay, you got it, you run it." And that was it. Even up in Red Cell, the Old Man didn't tell us how to do the ops. He says, "We need to get this guy. That's it, we need to get the job done." "Okay, Skipper." And we get the job done.

That's one thing that I really tried to do myself, tried to pass on. If I had eight guys on the team and one of them was the new guy, I want his opinion. Maybe he knows something, he's had some experience that might change something for us. He might have a new approach.

I learned that right from the Old Man. He let his enlisted men run the shop.

• • •

I love shooting and I love tactics, and I love being able to make a living doing it. I'm working with a company called GSGI, running direct operations—entry programs, what we call close-quarter conflicts. Making a decision process when you enter the door. That's primary.

GSGI's a training company, formed by a couple of Teams members about seven years ago. I ran into one of these guys when I was command master chief. They were filming *The Rock*, and they needed some people to go up and do the diving. I had about twelve guys who interviewed and they picked six of us. Once we got up there, they liked what we did, so they hired us as actors. We played the SEALs. Big stretch, huh?

So, after that I started working with GSGI, doing training on the weekends—just basic shooting courses.

This guy I was working with was talking about this training program and I said, "Sure, sounds great." So we started making it happen. We're pretty much on our way, getting a lot of business right now.

We started off with a lot of the suburban SWAT teams around LA. We've done the Border Patrol now, in San Diego, their react team and their instructors' course. We've done one correctional institute already and we've got about twenty more signed up. The Department of Energy called us. Let's see, who else? Customs called. El Paso Border Patrol. We're going to Indiana to do a SWAT team there next week. So, it's starting to cook.

I do the curriculum, put together all the training programs, which I feel good about because I'm putting my degree to use. I have a B.S. in workforce education. After I became command master chief out here at BUD/S, I finished up my class work in about two years and two months. So I did finally get my degree. It only took about twenty-five years, but I did it.

• • •

Looking at everything that's going on—especially in the Middle East right now, Korea—I think we need to get back to focusing on specialized units. We learned a lot, like up in Red Cell, about using one- and two-man teams. I believe there's a need for that now, to keep things going, the intel network, etc. Because, personally, I think the intel network they've got going today is not acceptable. They got people out there who aren't operators, so they don't know what they're looking for. And I don't think they're penetrated as deep as they could be. It's just not working like it should be.

And I see now, talking to some of the different agencies and police departments out there, the SpecWar folks might be doing some work inside the country as well. I'm just looking at possibilities for international terrorist groups penetrating the borders, and it's definitely out there.

When it comes to the Teams—well, right now, they're working on Vision 2001, which is a new training program. When I went through, there was really no time to go to school. So now they're trying to incorporate academics some, update the individuals not only academically but also in real-world situations. They'll give different classes, update them on the political side of the house, educate them that way.

The Teams are undermanned, like they've always been. But I can see them—well, I'm not going to say they're gonna do away with the Teams, but I can see them cutting down.

• • •

Training to build leaders, training to lead teams, that's something most corporations really don't do on their own. I had the opportunity to give a speech on motivation for a mortgage company out here, and they called me up again to give another one. So there is a need. Corporations really have no concept about teamwork. They're so focused on the individuals.

I mean, don't get me wrong—everybody looks for personal gain. But, if you really want to get the most personal gain, then get a good team together. You're gonna benefit more than trying to work by yourself and go out and do everything by yourself.

And so when I talked to these business people, that's what I talked about—motivation and teamwork and no individualism. Working together. It all goes back to my sea daddies, Dick and the others. They've taught me a lot, and I go back and say, "Here's what I learned." I want to pass that down.

Steve Hartman

aka Stevie Wonder

Once upon a time, I was walking from the Pentagon to my geographical bachelor pad when a silly-looking sailor, a dead ringer for Howdy Doody, asked me, "Where the fuck is BuPers?" From where he was standing, I knew he could smell it; he could spell it; he could even say it. He just couldn't see it because of the high-rise apartments in the way. He was wearing the submarine dolphins, so I knew he was lost up on the surface and desperate enough to resort to extreme measures, i.e., talking to strangers.

I had mercy on the poor slob and, in my polite Rogue way, gave him directions. I never had any indication that he and I would cross paths again, or that he'd become my beloved Stevie Wonder.

Actually, Steve started out on the Teams as "Boy Blunder." He earned that tag during his trial by fire before he was accepted in Red Cell as a "non-qual." The Team guys have hearts of gold, but they can have tongues of battery acid.

Why did I select Boy Blunder? I needed a diverse group of dirtbags to penetrate Red Cell's assigned targets. And Hartman was diverse. He was a mechanic; machinist mate; rifleman; bona fide dirtbag; New Yorker from LOOOOONG Island; a wiseass Irishman and arrogant asshole. Doesn't that combination just make you pop your nuts?

It was obvious to me that Steve couldn't spell career—he only understood teamwork and operations. So he passed performance, but flunked judgment—in most eyes, anyway. One nice thing about a Marine mentality is that you can count on them to perform their mission—and only their mission. I gave Steve the green light to seek new techniques or networks; I knew he'd work within the strategic overview I gave him. Not that he was timid; he just wanted to make sure he was providing worthwhile information, data we could actually use.

Wonder has limited language skills, although he is fluent in "New York." (He can use the word fuck as a verb, noun, pronoun, adjective, adverb, subject, object, indirect object, pluperfect progressive article—all in one sentence.) Because he'd been a Marine and served in the Navy's submarine force, he brought those two vital "languages" to our tool kit. We'd need to know the Standard Operational Procedures of both organizations to identify and exploit their vulnerabilities.

Stevie is smart as hell, although it took him a while to show it academically. He needed to experience the challenge of the real world to figure out what academic pursuits were worth his efforts. I know by now you've seen other evidence of this trait in the Real Team members. They weren't dumb; they just couldn't see how high school civics or college psych could benefit them. Their focus changed with some "hands-on" experience.

And, like the other Team guys, Steve needed the freedom to do his job without interference. No problem. Life is too short, and the mission is too important, to stifle talent for the sake of bureaucratic convenience and sanctity. That goes for the corporate world, too. If we're going to be competitive in a fast-changing environment, then we have to use every source of talent and initiative we can harness.

"Boy Blunder" made it through the welcome-aboard

hazing to become "Stevie Wonder." He was a true operational asset to Red Cell. Once he found a home in the Navy, he developed in a broad spectrum of operational areas to make sure he was a tried and tested asset. He's always been a big believer in achieving success through intense, realistic training. That made him a sound instructor for the FNGs who followed him. His flaws? Well, like me and a lot of other guys in this book, he was on leave when they handed out patience. This is especially true when Wonder is surrounded by incompetent assholes.

Today Steve is my VP for SOS Temps Inc. Right now, he's up to his ass in trying to get our new project, CrossRoads Training and Development Center, off the ground. He keeps me apprised of the efforts, or lack of same, in getting this project operational at the level we demand. In his spare time, he instructs, chases technological advances for security work enhancements, keeps the computer system at state-of-the-art or beyond, plays uncle to fourteen (soon fifteen) nieces and nephews, and spoils his German shepherd bitch, Sheeba. Wonder is not just Team—he's family!

NAME: **Steve Hartman**

DOB: **February 21, 1955**

HOMETOWN: **Huntington, New York**

MILITARY: **USMC Force Recon, Engineer Battalion, Maintenance Battalion. USN: USS *Finback;* USS *Hammerhead;* Navy**

Security Detachment,
Washington D.C.; Washington
Navy Yard. SPEC TEAM: Red
Cell

HIGHEST RANK: USMC: Staff sergeant. USN:
First class petty officer

SPECIALTY: USMC: Primary—force recon;
Secondary—motor transport
and maintenance chief. USN:
Machine maintenance

CURRENT: Vice president, SOS Temporary
Services

I'll make this teamwork bullshit real simple. It's about training, training, training. And leadership, leadership, leadership. And don't talk to me about "management." You can manage time, you can manage money, you can manage materials. You can't manage people.

• • •

I was the oldest kid—the experimental child. Parents always make their mistakes on their first kid. It was a real postwar baby-boomer family. Dad worked—he was an electrician—and Mom stayed home with the kids. There were seven of us—me, four brothers, and two sisters—so that was enough of a job. My dad fought in World War II, in the Army, but he never talked about it. No war stories at all. I don't even know what rank he was, anything.

I was a good kid, straight A student, until junior high. That's when I started getting rebellious. School didn't make sense anymore, what they were trying to teach us. So I spent more and more time racing—that's what I really wanted to do. Race cars, work on cars. I wanted to go to vocational school, be a mechanic, but my father didn't go for that. He wanted something else for me, something "better" than that, I guess. I know they did their best, but back then, especially, parents really wanted their kids to move up in the world, go to college, be a professional. And it didn't matter all that much what the kid wanted.

I spent as much time as I could racing, and working to get money for racing. I always had a job. Early on, I cut lawns and shoveled snow. I had my first real job when I was twelve—dishwasher at a restaurant. Then I worked in gas stations and did gofer work at a speed shop so I could learn more about racing, spend more time working on cars. My last job was with a tree company—pruning trees, spraying them, cutting them down. I made a lot of money on that job—more money than my father was making, which was another reason for him to be pissed off at me.

Finally, when I was seventeen, I got kicked out of high school. I *said* I was rebellious. I decided to join the Marines, just to get the hell out, and I spent seven years in the Corps.

• • •

I hate war stories—"Oh, let me tell you about the time I got ten of those SOBs," that kind of thing. Combat's not about having stories to tell at the bar.

Combat's about doing what it takes to accomplish your mission, to stay alive. And you'd better pray you had good training, because that's the only thing that's gonna get you through.

My first experience of combat was in Laos—1972, during the buildup in South Vietnam. I was eighteen years old, and it was my very first posting, part of a four-man team. We were all FNGs—E-nothings in the Marine Corps. We just did what we were told.

Our mission was what they called direct action—to disrupt NVA supply lines. They were running sampans on a couple of tributaries of the Mekong, and we were supposed to take 'em out. So we put together our plan and head out. Unfortunately, the intelligence we were given wasn't worth a shit. That's often the way intelligence goes, which is why it's a good idea to gather your own. Anyway, four days out we ran into the NVA where there weren't supposed to be any NVA. That was our first taste of a real live firefight.

What was that like? Hell, it was scary. This was not training. These were real bullets coming across at us, and they were trying to kill us—for real. Name of the game is survival. How bad do you want to live?

I guess we wanted to live more than they did. We killed more of them than they killed of us—they didn't kill any of us. But we got out of Dodge quick. We fell back, regrouped, kept going. Blew up a whole sampan convoy.

We worked like clockwork, and I attribute that to the amount and intensity of training we got. We had trust via the intense training. Part of that training is developing a team, working as a team. You've got to have that established before you go anywhere. And we were a good team. We took turns on the shit jobs, and divvied up the duties. If you carried the radio on the last op, somebody else gets it on the next op. It wasn't like there was one leader all the time—all of us would come up with ideas, resolve conflicts. It was pretty even.

I think we worked so well together because: A, we trusted each other, and B, things got pretty wild and hairy. There wasn't time for bullshit. You're scared and you've got a job to do. You can't focus on the fear, or you'll never accomplish anything. You'll just freeze. So you have to control the fear—respect it, respect your adversary. Know his capabilities better than he does. And just do it.

Fear is a good thing. It keeps you alert. It keeps you alive. You can do a lot of things when you're scared.

Working in a small team like that, you do it all, and you learn pretty fast what you're good at, what's easy, and what you gotta work at. The op functions I liked best are walking point, shooting, and demolition. The thing I liked about walking point was the way it focuses you. You have to detect the bad guys before they get you. Outsmart them before they have a chance to fuck you up.

I hate swimming. I mean, I just hate it. Of course, you've got to do a lot of it on the Teams. So you just don't think about it. It's something you've got to do to get to the target—so you just gotta do it.

That was a tremendous time in my life, but I

wouldn't want to go back and do it again. Leave that to the young guys.

Now, *if* I got to help pick the team, and *if* we got paid what we ought to get paid, I would go out on missions like the shit Dick writes about in the novels. Those are two big ifs. But, yeah, I'd do that for damn sure.

• • •

The biggest difference between the Marine Corps and the Navy is the leadership. The Navy has no real leadership. The Marine officers stick up for their men—I mean, really stick up for them. The troops eat first, and the officers eat last. That's just the way they think of it.

In the Navy it's just the opposite. The Navy officers have this mightier-than-thou attitude—not all of them, but most of them. That's how they're trained at Annapolis. And that's the culture that develops, and that's what's rewarded. Navy officers, for the most part, don't lead from the front. They lead for their own convenience and to punch their own ticket. I never had a problem telling guys like that, "If it wasn't for us, you wouldn't be worth shit."

When I was a sergeant in the Marine Corps, twenty years old, I had more responsibility, more men under me, than a lot of chiefs on submarines. I had to learn to motivate, to lead guys who were older than I was, who had more experience. I didn't take any bullshit, but I was fair. I expected things to be done, and I didn't want to hear any excuses.

I'm not saying the Navy's a total disaster. The second submarine I was on was a good sub. They had a good CO, they had a good XO, and the crew was pretty tight. So they did a lot of good work.

The first sub—that was another story. There was absolutely no sense of a team, nobody pulling together on a mission. The XO was the biggest problem there. He wouldn't let it happen. His ego got in the way of everything—and why he was so goddamn impressed with himself, I have no idea. He tried to micromanage every division in the submarine— wouldn't let us do our jobs. I hated it. I was way ahead in the qualifications timetable and I was qualified on more watch stations than anybody else on board. And this asshole's trying to tell me what to do? Man, I do not tolerate that well.

I was one of about six guys to get kicked off the sub at the same time. The XO sent me to a doctor because he said I was crazy. The doctor did me a favor. He talked to me for a while and I told him all about it— how I was just fed up with the bullshit. Finally he asked me how I'd blow up the submarine. And I went, "What? How would I *what?*"

He said, "Just answer the question."

"Well, give me a half hour and I could send that thing to the moon."

He just smiled. "You'll be off that sub this afternoon." And I was.

Then the commodore of the squadron called me in. It was about a month before I finally got in to see him, and the first thing he did was apologize for taking so long to see me. I just said, "Well, Commodore, I'm an

E-3 and you're an O-6—there's a little bit of a difference there."

Basically, what he had to say was, "I wanted to talk to you because you're not wet behind the ears and you can tell me what's going on there." So I told him—I said that submarine's a disaster, and I told him exactly why. He really listened. Eventually, that XO was sent to the Navy Yard—I don't know where he finally ended up. Don't much care, as long as I don't have to deal with him.

That commodore was smart—a good leader. You expect a leader to get out there and find out what's really going on. Leaders don't just sit behind a desk, reading memos and trying to find out about their business from the *Wall Street Journal*. If you want to be a real leader, you've got to get out there and get the heartbeat of the company and the heartbeat of the troops. You got to get out there and actually talk to people.

You don't have to have a CEO who's down in the mailroom every day. Of course they've got to delegate. A leader's got to be able to do two things: surround himself with the right people, and ask the right questions. No one individual can run an organization. Anyone who thinks he can is nuts.

● ● ●

I'd heard about Dick years before I ever met him. When I was in Thailand in the Marine Corps, we'd see all the cable traffic about what was going on in the region, so I was aware of what he was doing over in Cambodia. I was aware of it, and interested.

Then, years later, in 1983, I was in Washington, looking for the NMPC—the Naval Military Personnel Center at the Navy Annex. I had some paperwork to fill out or some such bullshit. So I ran into this guy on the street, this big ugly Navy officer, and I asked him for directions to the NMPC. I don't remember exactly what he said, something really smart-ass.

Well, my attitude on that is that if you can dish it out, you better be able to take it. I don't give a shit if you're an officer or not. So I said something smart right back and he finally told me where the NMPC was.

So that's the first time I met Dick.

Then, about a year later, I went to work for him on Red Cell.

• • •

Being part of the Teams was like going home. After all those years in the Navy, it was fantastic. The Teams are warriors. Community, loyalty, dedication. And anything goes.

It was hard, stepping into a Team. I mean, these guys had all worked together, a lot of them had gone through training together. And I'd washed out of BUD/S. I went through when I was thirty-one years old, which is pretty damn old for that kind of bullshit. I got rolled out on a medical for my feet. I've always had busted-up feet, and I'd made it through seven years in the Marines and three years in the Navy by just doing it. Just gut it up and go. But the clock ran out on me in BUD/S.

So I really had to prove myself to the other guys on Red Cell. I had to pay my dues. I knew what to expect. For instance, I wasn't as good with the pistols at first, so I bought a lot of beer. That's just the way it is. I had no problem with it.

And then, early on, my function was intel work, setting up the black programs. That meant I wasn't going on the road. The first mission I went on was a two-week terrorist exercise on a Naval base in the Philippines. That's when the door started to open. But it didn't open all the way on that first trip. It takes time to prove yourself. You just don't walk in and say, "I'm here, ready to go to work" and expect a group of guys like that to just pull you right in and say, "Okay, fine. Come on in, we're so glad you're here." It doesn't work that way. I went through it, everybody goes through it. I watched the guys from the West Coast come in, and man, was I relieved. They didn't shoot as well as they should have, so I didn't have to buy as much beer anymore.

See, you can't just say, "Yeah, I can go through the door. I can handle that." Don't tell me. *Show* me. I want to know you're going to be there when the shit hits the fan. And until I've seen that, words don't mean diddly.

The great thing about working with Dick is that he lets you loose. He lets me use my creativity, shall we say. That makes all the difference. On Red Cell we'd get a mission and develop an op plan, then we'd brief him and the other officers. We'd tell them everything, down the line: this is how we're going to insert, this is how we're going to hit the target, this is how we're going to extract. Dick always asked a million questions, playing Mr. Murphy. If he liked what we were doing, if we could justify everything, he'd say, "Do it." And we were on our way. "See ya, boss—be back later."

There was none of this bullshit of making changes just to make changes—to show he was the boss. He knew we could do it, and he let us do it. All we had to do was keep him aware of what was going on—especially if there was a fuck-up. Man, I got my ass chewed a number of times. But with Dick—with a good leader—there's the ass chewing, and then it's over and done with, move along. Maybe he'll bust your balls a little later, but he assumes you've learned what you needed to learn. He doesn't use it as an excuse to keep looking over your shoulder, getting in your way.

In the Navy, and even now, I'd have to deal with these boneheads who try to micromanage everything. I used to tell people—officers, whoever—"Let me do my job, or get out of my face. If you don't think I can do this, then relieve me."

And it goes back to trust. If you feel like someone doesn't even trust you to do one simple thing, they're not ever going to trust you on the big things.

• • •

The best briefing I ever saw was on CNN during the Gulf War. This Marine general was telling his company, "When we finally do start fighting, all this mom-and-apple-pie goes out the window. The truth of the matter is you're going to be fighting for one another. You're going to be fighting for the guy you've been training with for the last two years, that you've been working with for the last three years. That's who you're gonna be fighting for."

That's the best briefing I ever heard from any officer. Because he told the truth.

People aren't stupid. They know when they're being lied to. When a business has a crisis, they may try to put a spin on it, put up a smoke screen. But the ones that get through the crisis best are the ones that come straight out and say, "This is what the problem is, this is what we're doing to fix it."

And you know if a company is honest with its customers, it's more likely to be honest with its employees. And, again, it goes back to trust. Do you trust your boss to go to bat for you? Does he trust you to do your job? If you don't have that basic trust, you don't have a team.

• • •

I've said combat is a great learning tool—nothing better for getting your attention. But you don't have to be in a combat situation to mold a good team. You look for good people—people who work hard, who are willing to learn. It's just that the focus is different. Now you're focusing on business—you bring the same intensity level to a different area. The competition is the enemy. Cut and dried. How do you beat the enemy? Then you develop your strategy off that.

I do think that military experience gives you an advantage in business. Most people who go into the military are intense at the outset. They strongly believe in what they believe. And they don't take no for an answer. Then the flexibility you learn, the adaptability—the ability to think on your feet—you bring that right along with you. And you learn to be adaptable because you train like hell.

It all comes down to training. Technology has changed things so much, changed things so fast, and continues to change things so fast, that you've got to work at staying on top. Especially in business. Time and distance—they almost don't exist anymore, because information travels so fast. Unless you're on top of your business and unless you know what your competition is doing on a daily basis, you're going to get behind the power curve.

Look at AT&T. Their demise is their own fault. They were complacent in their position in the marketplace. On top of that, they pay their CEO $14 million and then they turn around and lay off fifty thousand people. Now where is the sense in that?

The ivory tower culture in a lot of large companies—the AT&Ts, the GMs—that's very tough to change. You'd really have to strip it and start over at the top. That's where the problem lies. It's not the people who are actually doing the work. Everyone wants to do a good job—but they want to be rewarded for that good job. It's like everything else—you show loyalty, you want loyalty back. It's give and take.

• • •

I'm still working with Dick—I'm VP of SOS Temporary Services, a security company. I run all the training, all that happy, good bullshit. I deal with a lot of Dick's fan mail, too. And I set up the Rogue Warrior Web page.

Probably the biggest project we're working on right now is the CrossRoads Training Center. It's a huge complex in Indiana, right in the middle of the country—the crossroads, right?—and it's designed to help build better leaders in corporate America. We'll introduce leadership, team building, and motivational programs, using a combination of classroom work and physical tools to teach people how to lead and how to work in a team.

It's not superstrenuous; we're not trying to kill anybody. This isn't a military situation at all. But the physical activity is going to have a lot more impact on people than just sitting in a classroom, staring at a blackboard, filling out papers. Think about those three-day seminars people go to—what are they going to remember out of all the shit that's thrown at them? What's going to really impact them so they'll remember it, go back to it, and use it? What we're going to do at CrossRoads will have much more personal impact. It'll be something they can look back on and keep learning from, and it'll be fun at the same time. I mean, what's the best way to clear your head, get focused? You do something physical. Go for a walk, get some fresh air. We'll just take it up a notch, that's all.

We're also putting together a youth development package for kids fourteen to eighteen who're thinking about going into the military—sort of a prep school for kids who want a career in SEALs, Special Forces. It's a confidence builder and, again, a way for them to learn how to work in teams. That's what life's about. Not everybody is going to do what you want them to do, when you want them to do it. You can't just get frustrated, you can't just yell at him—you've got to figure out how to motivate him and get the job done.

And we're going to have a program specifically tailored for women. There are so many more women business leaders now, and no one's addressing this market. So our program will focus on confidence building, leadership, team building—a lot of the same things in the corporate program, but directed specifically to women, with women-only classes. There'll also be classes in shooting and rape prevention, some self-defense. It's a way to help women gain confidence in their abilities, including their physical abilities, which is something that still isn't being encouraged enough early on.

And finally, there'll be a separate shooting school and tactical training just for law enforcement officers.

It's a hell of a project, getting this thing going, but it's something that's really needed—something that nobody else is offering.

● ● ●

Like I said, I got kicked out of high school. I got my high school diploma while I was on active duty in the Marines. I completely skipped college. Two years ago, I got into a graduate-level program at Georgetown with just a high school diploma. They let me in with my résumé.

It was this intensive, six-month deal called the Ex-

ecutive Global Leadership Program. We studied executive leadership and strategy, global logistics, international law, business law, cross-cultural negotiations,
government business relations. There were twenty-
two people in the program, and all of them had at
least a master's degree. All of them except me. But
these weren't ivory-tower academic types. They were
business people—an executive from Mobil Oil, a few
people who'd started consulting businesses, a network news editor. A lot of very smart people.

It was intense. An unbelievable amount of work.
But I finished up with a 4.0. Steve Hartman, Mr.
Honor Grad. Pretty damn hard to believe, isn't it?

● ● ●

The world situation today is worse than during the
Cold War—more unstable. There are more nationalis-
tic conflicts today than ever before, because the Soviet
Union controlled a lot of those conflicts and now
they're gone. And there's a lot less control on the
nukes in Russia, as opposed to the Soviet Union.
They'd have you believe differently, but I can tell you
that's not true.

Then there's China—if we don't get a grasp on
that situation, we're going to be in big trouble fifteen
or twenty years from now. You got Iran, you got
Iraq—all of these regional conflicts that just keep sim-
mering.

Take the Balkans. If they pull the U.S. troops out,
that place will blow up again. If the United States
stays in and they start playing hardball diplomati-
cally, they might solve the problem. I hated to see the

troops go over there, but there wasn't any other option. If we hadn't gone in, there'd have been a replay of the scenario that led to World War I.

As far as Iraq—all the saber rattling doesn't do any good. What they're talking about now, the air strikes, that's not going to solve the problem. *[Steve's right, and here's why. Air strikes just create some bomb damage; the most they can do is delay the delivery of weapons. That's just a temporary setback. If we were really concerned, we'd take out Saddam. You see a threat, you cut off its head. You don't just nibble at its foot. All we're doing is giving Saddam a chance to get points in the Muslim world for sticking his finger in America's eye and getting away with it. We have no balls and he's got big ones. Plus, he has nothing to lose.]* If I were in charge, I'd go after Saddam's money. Cut off his cash directly, wherever you can. Then set up an aid program that goes directly to the people. Fly the food and the supplies in, then let the U.N. or some aid organization oversee the distribution. Keep it out of the hands of the Iraqi government. Go after the hearts and minds of the people. The sanctions we've got now are just hurting the people.

Same thing in Cuba. The sanctions have got Castro in a box, but who cares? Who's he going to affect? He's got no power. It boils down to politics—the fact that the Cuban-American community in Florida has a lot of votes, a lot of money, a lot of clout.

And that's the basic problem with our foreign policy, or government policy in general. None of these politicians has the balls to stand up and say, "What we're doing is wrong and this is what I'm going to do to remedy the situation." Being a real leader calls for courage—knowing what's got to be done and having the guts to get it done. Politicians today might know what's needed, but they're not going to do it unless it's politically expedient, unless it polls well. I say, fuck polls. Just lead.

I've seen so much of this in the Navy. When push comes to shove, politics will take precedence over mission. Officers will take a look at their own career path, not the overall mission. Officers don't stay operational long enough these days. To get ahead, they've got to move on to staff jobs and start punching that ticket, looking out for their next promotion.

And that's the biggest problem I see with the armed forces, and the Teams, today. Kids today are great. They're bigger, they're stronger, they're smarter. But they're not being utilized the way they should because of the leadership. And that affects the retention rates.

Officers are rotated too much, rotated out of operational command too fast. And the go-getters get hammered down. And we're talking about the *military*—in that line of work, you'd better be aggressive, or you're dead.

That has got to change. With the world situation the way it is, the military is going to have to focus more on SpecOps. Unconventional warfare—small unit packages that aren't part of a major operation. It's not just us/them, United States/USSR anymore. There are a million different little conflicts all over the world. Look at where U.S. troops are deployed now. They haven't been used this much since World War II. I call it the USPD now—the United States Police Department. I don't think that's what anybody signs up for when they go into the armed forces.

Harry Humphries

aka Harry the Hump

Harry is a New Jersey boy who wandered into the Navy, then the Teams; he's still part of the Special Warfare family today. Harry didn't serve with me in SEAL Team SIX or Red Cell, but I still consider him part of the Team. He and his wife, Cathy, hosted us in all our visits to Southern California; that alone is a major commitment. Harry enjoyed meeting the "new breed," and they looked forward to getting the dirt on some of our escapades in Vietnam. Harry's place was like a safe house for us, a place where we knew we'd be uninterrupted and unharassed. We always stayed long beyond what anyone would consider socially acceptable. The morning after always looked like someone had chucked a grenade in the house, with snoring stinking SEAL bodies sprawled all over the house and backyard.

I consider Harry one of my true brothers. In combat, Harry and I communicated without uttering a word or wasting time with hand signals; we were that much in sync. Today, many years later, we do the same in business negotiations or training events. When we're interviewed together, on any subject, we're Huntley & Brinkley, Thump & Thud, Muck & Mire, Arts & Crafts, Barbell & Dumbbell, Frick & Frack. After all these years, we're still a Team.

Harry was always a true operator, motivated by love of mission and love of country. He gave up a lucrative and luxurious lifestyle to follow his heart and rejoin his Team on their deployment to Vietnam. (His mother always *blamed me for yanking him out of the family business to go frolic in combat.*) Personal gain has never been a high priority. Even today, running GSGI, he gets his greatest reward from sharing his expertise, helping current operators hone their skills to be better prepared to perform their missions.

Harry started out as an engineer, and he remains an engineer in his approach. He takes on every situation methodically—analyzes it, develops a plan, then executes that plan in a totally professional manner. No wild-hair-up-the-ass, shoot-from-the-hip bullshit from Harry.

The negative side? Do not expect him to return your phone call immediately; he's too fucking busy. Do not expect him to criticize your performance; he'll look for the silver lining every time. Do not expect to get him past a single goddamn gadget-and-gizmo booth at a trade show. That's the engineer in him—always looking for a way to make a better mousetrap, while I just want to blow up the traps and the fucking mice. Together we have fun and get shit done.

One thing Harry fails to mention—he's a genuine Hollywood mogul. He works with producer Jerry Bruckheimer on both big-screen and made-for-TV productions; he's riding herd on the movie progress of Rogue Warrior, one of Jerry's productions. Harry has helped expose his teammates to Hollywood, and Hollywood to the true character of the Teams—a true win-win situation. Harry's always trying improve his teammates' visibility in show biz, finding ways for them to parlay their experience into employment there or with GSGI. Even though he's been out of the Teams for years, his heart's still with the guys.

NAME:	Harry Humphries
DOB:	November 17, 1940
HOMETOWN:	Kearney, New Jersey
MILITARY:	U.S. Naval Reserve; USS *Malloy*; UDTR; UDT 22; SEAL Team TWO
HIGHEST RANK:	E-6; first-class petty officer
SPECIALTY:	Weapons and demolition
CURRENT:	Founder and director, GSGI (Global Study Group, Inc.), Tactical Training and Consulting

With respect to the SEAL program, Vietnam was not the beginning of anything. It was just another job we had. We'd done black operations in Cuba; we had done things that we still don't talk about. So some of us had seen combat, had been shot at and shot back before. But certainly Vietnam was, still is, the most sustained period of constant combat the Teams experienced.

I don't care what kind of training you go through—and we had the best there is—no matter what you go through in the training environment, until you test yourself in the field of fire, you don't know. Are you able to do it? Are you good at it? You don't know that until you go through it. That's the big *if*—"How am I going to operate under fire?" Once you prove that to yourself, then things become a lot different. You actually go through tremendous character changes. Some for the better, some for the worse. The point is, you get up every day, getting ready to do your job, and you look at yourself in the mirror, you're putting your cammie on your face and so on, and you're thinking to yourself, "This could be my last day." That's the way you learn how to live. Every day is a major football game. More than a football game, because coming back is not a guaranteed thing.

• • •

A lot of my relatives, uncles and so forth, were in World War II, mostly in the Army. They all did the usual World War II thing, served their time and got out. There was one uncle who talked quite a bit about his experiences. He had attended a military prep school, the Admiral Farragut Academy. He was kind of a role model for me. What he talked about was the military and one's obligation to the military. Remember, we're talking Second World War now. I always found that to be quite an honorable thing. Thus my desire to get involved in the Naval Academy at a very early age. I was still in grammar school when I decided I was going to be a plebe, go to the same prep school he did.

My dad was a production manager for a chemical processing facility, the family business. My mother took care of me and my sisters, and she also did the entrepreneur thing—she had a shop in the summertime.

Class 26 UDTIR 1960. "Day #1 of the rest of my life."
The Rogue Warrior is front row, standing, second from right. *Richard Marcinko*

Dan Capel. "Ah—the peace and quiet of a small war." *Richard Marcinko*

Steven Seigel. "Leadership evolving—the transition from enlisted to commissioned ranks."

Steven Seigel

Larry Barrett. "Come on down!" *Richard Marcinko*

The Rogue Warrior and Harry Humphries. *Richard Marcinko*

Norm Carley. "God, it feels good when I lead with my face."

Richard Marcinko

Dave Tash (right) with wife, Gretchen, and Misty.

Dave Tash

Denny Chalker, SEAL Team Six, during a training evolution at Camp A. P. Hill, Virginia. "Wonder if anyone ever thought we were just revolutionaries in the wrong place?"

Kevin Dockery

Harry Humphries. "Humphries at sea."
Richard Marcinko

Al Tremblay. "Hell, I had to kill something."
Richard Marcinko

(Left to right) Purdy, Chalker, McNabb, Marcinko, Mink, and Prusaic. "We kick ass with a smile on our faces."
Richard Marcinko

Larry Barrett, Steve Hartman, and the Rogue Warrior. "The well is deep at the Rogue Manor Gin Mill."

Richard Marcinko

Class 26 UDTIR, twenty-eight years later.

Richard Marcinko

Chris Caracci and Nancy Marcinko. "When the boss is gone—just "Blow them Away." *Richard Marcinko*

My son, Matthew Loring. "Comin' out of the bush."
Richard Marcinko

Matthew Loring. "When I push this button— you all die."
Richard Marcinko

Class 26 UDTIR, thirty years later. *Richard Marcinko*

The Rogue Warrior.
"Stay off the property—
trespassers shot.
Survivors shot again."

Richard Marcinko

There was pressure on me from day one to go into the family business. I always liked engineering and mathematics and so forth, so that's what I studied, but I really wanted to serve.

• • •

There was some German spoken in my family; my grandfather was a second-generation immigrant. I actually went to Portuguese language school while I was in the SEAL Team, but German I picked up in school after I got out of the Navy. I worked for a German-based international company, Henkel Corporation. I was the first American to go over as a technical auditor. I was stationed in Düsseldorf, and of course I had to learn to speak and write the language. My family background gave me an ear for it, and I'm sure that made it a little easier to learn.

• • •

Admiral Farragut Naval Academy is basically a prep school for the military Naval Academy. I was in the Naval Reserve at the age of seventeen, because they had a Reserve unit attached to the school. I had several two-week tours on Naval vessels during my summer cruise periods. The Naval Science department at Admiral Farragut actually was run by Navy chiefs and one Naval officer, so it was considered a Navy school command. The Reserve program was there to offer unlimited appointments to the Naval Academy for students at the school who wished to go that route, as opposed to having to get appointments through senators or congressmen. And that was my original intention, to go on to the Naval Academy and go in as a commissioned officer in the United States Navy.

But in my four years at Admiral Farragut Academy, I did quite well in sports, in basketball, football, and track, and I was offered football scholarships to several universities. Having done four years of very rigid Naval discipline in prep school, I was ready for the other side of the fence. I kind of got a smell of the outside, where there were actually women, these people in skirts, instead of dungarees. I thought I'd give that a shot. It was probably the biggest mistake of my life, but I had fun trying it, anyway.

• • •

I ended up going to Rutgers University and playing football for them for a while. From Rutgers, I went to Monmouth College, where they specialized in the kind of electronics that I was interested in. From there, I wound up on active duty with my Naval Reserve unit.

We were called up on active duty during the Berlin Wall crisis—as soon as the wall went up, there was an immediate call for Reserves. My unit was called in for about a six-month period, and I had an obligatory two-year active duty to serve anyway. So since they'd basically screwed up the first semester of my senior year, I decided to stay active. I figured I'd finish up my two years, then get out and finish school. It took more than two years, but I did finally finish that degree.

• • •

I was on a destroyer escort, DE 791, USS *Malloy*, attached to the underwater sound lab in New London,

Connecticut. We conducted development work for variable depth sonar, which was a new concept back then. It was a highly electronic-oriented mission, and with my engineering and electronics background, I was a natural fit for it.

That was when I first had exposure to Navy diving, Navy divers, some UDT guys. Up until then, I had no idea such a thing existed. So I heard all the stories about all these great guys and the superhuman things they could do, the kind of stunts they sort of cavalierly pulled off for laughs. That sounded like a neat thing.

The ship deployed constantly, because our tasking was very, very strong, and I was looking to get off the vessel. At the time, BuPers had an annual or biannual call for volunteers to go to UDTR, Underwater Demolition Team Replacement training—this was before BUD/S. I saw that as a way to get out of the fleet. I volunteered for UDTR—and kept on volunteering. They didn't want to let me go, because I was in a critical electronic rate; after all, they had an engineer, basically, an electronics engineer working in the fire control section. They didn't want to lose me. So it took me seven chits to get off the vessel.

During the Cuban blockade, I finally got permission to leave the vessel, and that was only because I did something that saved the captain's butt. Basically, we lost a piece of equipment over the side of the vessel. We had a piece of extremely expensive experimental electronics equipment, which we'd submerged on a cable, and somehow we'd managed to walk the fantail of the vessel over the cable, trapping the cable with the screws of the ship. We were dead in the water, at sea, and if we cut the cable, we'd lose that expensive equipment.

I went to the captain and said, "Look, let me go over the side, sir." I put some Jack Brown diving gear on, which was on every Naval vessel, designed for damage control. It was about three in the morning, in the Atlantic Ocean. I went over the side, saw that the device was within reasonable view. I walked down the cable and saw that I could in fact unshackle the cable and attach the equipment to something else. So I went up to the surface and got an auxiliary cable to bring down, and I shackled the auxiliary onto the device. Then I disconnected it from the entangled cable, and up came this expensive device. Then I untangled the cable from the screws, and the ship was free.

The captain was very appreciative. He just wanted to know what I wanted—an attaboy in my file, and what else. I said, "Sir, I just want to have my chit to UDTR honored. If you could expedite that, I'd be most appreciative." The next day I got word from my buddy, one of the radiomen, that I'd just gotten my orders to go to UDT training. They dropped me off in Puerto Rico and then I went up to Little Creek, Virginia.

I was the first trainee to report. I was there months early, before training started, actually. There I was, stuck with all those instructors. They had their way with me, months before anyone else showed up. It was actually quite enjoyable.

• • •

I was in class 29. There's actually a book coming out called *Class 29*, by John Roat, who's one of my classmates, and he goes into a lot of detail about our experience. I think our class had 130 students, 150 students, maybe. We had an awful lot of foreign students in that class, for some reason. We had Greeks, we had Dutch commandos, we had Danish—not Danish pastries, but Danish sailors—we had Pakistanis, we had tons of foreign soldiers. Of course, that still goes on today. Nations that are friendly to the United States will put their troops through to crosstrain and pick up the skills taught by Naval Special Warfare.

We graduated some thirty students, I believe, a good third of which were foreigners. If they hadn't been there, I'd say we'd have graduated about twenty Americans.

In those days, there was a training class twice a year in Little Creek, Virginia, a winter class and a summer class. The same on the West Coast, in Coronado. Our class was the winter class that year. That means we were extremely, extremely cold and extremely, extremely wet. I think if I remember anything from those thirty-some years ago, it was being cold and wet. Then, of course, the fatigue and the physical aspects are still in the memory bank. But the one thing that stands out was how constantly cold I was and how constantly wet I was. How each day was like a year. At the end of every day, when I'd gotten through another one, I didn't even think about how many more. I just thought, "One more down. One more down," as I crawled into the rack.

As far as Hell Week went, that was just a five-day period of torture. It's your first wake-up call, what you can expect down the road. I think that's the one common thing that's unspoken, the thing that everyone who's gone through training will keep in the back of their minds—"I don't want to do that too often."

You reached a point where the physical stress was so great, or the mental aspects of having to go through something you absolutely did not want to do—it was hard to do it. You did it anyway. That happened over and over and over again. But all I had to do during those long, difficult runs on the beach was just look up and see the haze gray ships going out to sea, and I just started to run a little faster. I was not going back there.

• • •

I started out in UDT 22, which was where I met Dick, and then I was the first non-plankowner to come aboard SEAL Team TWO. I put in for that, when I realized what they were doing. It was just a question of getting a billet and getting accepted. At the time, the commanding officer was Tom Tarbox. He and I had played football together in the Navy amphibious team and we knew each other well, so I was accepted when an opening came up.

That's when I decided this was the place for me. I'd found my niche in life; these were the guys I wanted to be with. The professionalism, the degree of skill and silent pride, was exceptional. It was truly a great honor to be there. I still believe today that in those years the Teams were at their absolute peak in terms of quality of personnel and programming—although it was a formative period when Naval management had no idea what to do with these guys.

It was different then. I was twenty-five, twenty-six, and I was probably the youngest kid there. Typically you had to be in UDT several years before you went to a Team. You had to be career oriented—there were a lot of training funds being put to use, and they didn't want to spend the money on a four-year guy coming in and out. A lot of the guys had many years in the fleet even before they came to UDT. Back then, they were much more well-rounded individuals, in terms of knowing what the Navy was all about.

That all changed very quickly when the Vietnam period occurred. We were taking kids right out of training, sending them into platoons, training them up with their platoon mates and sending them over to Vietnam. The task was so great, the need was so great, that there was no time to filter, to get the kind of guys you had prior to Vietnam.

At one point, I had the option to go into the integration program and become an officer, which was the route Dick took, or I could stay where I was. I definitely did not want to leave the Teams. If I had to stay an E-6 for the rest of my Naval career, that was fine, as long as I was operating with the Teams.

The men were what it was all about. Certainly the task and the job were tremendously exciting, but the real issue was being with guys that were, without question, the greatest guys I'd ever known in my life. It was truly an honor to be a part of that group. I'd never seen such a quality of men, in such a tight unit. I had played sports, been on major football teams, the camaraderie and teamwork thing was not new to me, but to see this kind of quality all in one location was quite a treat.

I don't want to come across saying the guys who were in then were better than the guys who are in today. The quality of individual certainly hasn't changed. They were there for different reasons in the old days. Nobody knew what the hell a frogman was back then. They certainly didn't know what a SEAL was. Most of them went there sort of accidentally and fell in love with the life and the people they were working with. Today, an awful lot has been published about the Teams and what they are; I think there's more of an incentive to punch the ticket and say, "I've been there." Do the four years and get out. The shipping-over rate in the Teams now is around twenty percent. It was ninety-something when I was in. You got out when you retired. You got out because you had to. I was one of the only ones who got out, and I got out because I had a high-paying job waiting for me.

• • •

I did two tours in Southeast Asia. My first trip, I went with Dick in the Eighth Platoon when he went over for the second time. I had actually left the Teams, after going on an intelligence-gathering mission with Assault Group Two, which was conducted in France. I don't want to go into details, but that was the end of my first tour in SEAL Team. Then I found out that we had deployed to Southeast Asia. Well, there was no way I could stay behind. I could not live with myself. I had to get back with my platoon, had to get overseas and be with them.

So I pulled some strings, Dick pulled some strings in D.C., got me back to my rate so I didn't lose any income. It was as if I'd just gone to school for eleven months, because there I was, back on active duty again. I still hadn't had time to get off the twelve-o'clock-martini-lunch routine, and people are shooting at me and I've got to shoot back. I jumped off a helo and started charging a tree line, and I was thinking, "Isn't it time for lunch yet?" But I quickly got over that.

The second tour after that was with the Phoenix program. I went over as a PRU adviser for Long Xuyen province, near Can Tho. I was wounded severely in that assignment, and spent several months in the hospital. I guess it took me six months to get to operational duty with the Teams again. I had the option to take a medical discharge, or take my time getting back to active duty. Of course I only wanted one thing and that was to get back to the Teams. Within six months I was back, and I had jump status with the Teams. With a little bit of a limp, but it managed to disappear after a while.

From there, I took a training platoon for SEAL Team TWO, which trained up operational platoons getting ready to deploy to Vietnam. We had our own in-house training and preparedness program for our own operational units deploying. That was when I realized that I really enjoyed instructing.

• • •

The most difficult thing I did was get on the back of a jeep with a .50-caliber, me and two other guys, and go out into the city of Chau Duc, where there were thousands of Vietcong just waiting for us. We had to go through several miles of Vietcong-infested streets, fighting our way through with the .50, pocket after pocket of firefights, just sitting ducks on that jeep truck. We had to get to an area where American nurses, civilians, were being held captive, break into that area, kill everyone around them, and get them out alive, throw them in the back of the jeep, and fight our way back out through the city. There's no way we should have made that alive, but we all did.

It can only be because of pure luck. Luck and audacity. Mostly luck. And we went because it had to be done.

We were in the city, Dick was there, too, and we heard about the nurses. An Army sergeant with the PRU advisory department said, "I'm going in." I said, "You're not going in without me." I asked Dick if I could go in, and he said, "Yeah." He wasn't happy about it, but he realized the position. Two other SEALs got on the jeep with me and off we went. There was no plan—we just went.

One guy was driving the jeep, and I'm on the .50-caliber machine gun on the back, firing away. There's pockets of people shooting at us. I notice that the jeep was really being driven professionally. I mean, this thing is going from one side of the street to the other. It was impossible to hit us because the jeep was moving so erratically. This guy really knew what he was doing, driving this jeep, and I was really impressed. All of a sudden, we're coming up on a bridge and the jeep is heading directly for the abutment, getting ready to careen into it and go over the side. I'm thinking the driver might have been hit, so I look down. That's when I realize what was going on all that time. I'm firing this .50 right over the driver's head, blowing his eardrums out. He had to keep putting his hands over his ears. He'd never touched the steering wheel since we'd started out. That was the explanation for that expert driving. By the time we got to the bridge we were out of the danger zone, so he could take his hands off his ears and start driving.

• • •

Dick and I became instant friends when we first met each other in UDT 22. We'd both gone up together for the integration program and took the test for it together. I was Naval Reserve and not eligible when I took the test, but no one was aware of that, believe it or not. Our record keeping wasn't all that great. Anyway, Dick left UDT 22 to go to OCS and do his sea time before he could get back to the Teams. I went over to SEAL Team TWO about the time he went over to get his commission. He'd just gotten back to SEAL Team TWO when we'd come back off that French intelligence trip.

There was a definite agreement in our personalities. We were two peas in a pod. Where he may be a little more big picture than I am, I may be a little more pragmatic than he is. But there was a balancing, if you will, of the two personalities. We've been the best of friends ever since, and that was thirty-five years ago.

It's very difficult to have a friendship and a command situation at the same time, but Dick is able to do that because of the type of leader he is. He's not a micromanager. He gives the people under him the credit for having intelligence and decision-making capability. He treats everyone as an equal until they prove they're not, then he takes a different position with them. But our relationship, as friends and command/subordinate, has always been driven by mutual respect.

●   ●   ●

After I got out of the Navy, I went into the family business for a couple of years. Then I decided I didn't want to work for the family any longer and saw there was no future in that, so I went on and did my own things. I wound up working for Henkel as an operational security/operational auditor, if you will. Spent five or six years with them. That's where I started to get my security background, counterterrorism awareness, that type of thing. Got out of that, and wound up instructing and consulting in counterterrorism security issues, which is what I do today. I train tactical, military, and federal law enforcement agencies in counterterrorist tactics and general high-speed SWAT tactics.

When I was doing the training for SEAL Team TWO, that's when I realized I enjoyed instructing, passing along the skills I'd acquired. That's always been my most desired function. I hung up my engineer's hat and put on my instructor's hat and have been happier than hell ever since.

I've always been a crusader. I believe there's a right and a wrong in this world, and I believe the right needs to win. If the right side isn't made strong enough, the wrong will win. Anything I can do to prevent that from happening, that's what I strive to do.

I'm always involved in something. I just came back from Kosovo and Albania, trying to see what I could do to help over there. I'm on my way to Colombia. I enjoy teaching what needs to be taught to young men and young women who are fighting for the right side. One person is one person. But if that one person is giving knowledge to thousands and thousands of others—in essence, he's deploying with those individuals. If you've got the knowledge and the support—and I've always surrounded myself with the best talent I can find—then as a unit you're going to go do a good job in getting the knowledge out there.

• • •

Instilling teamwork is really out of my realm. If the teamwork is there, and that's up to the individual team leaders, then it's there. If it's not there—and I see those where the teamwork doesn't exist—the operations suffer. But my job is to teach a specialized skill to a given unit. The skills we teach are much higher speed and much more advanced than what they would get through a normal police training outfit. We are teaching federal agencies. We have scheduled military programs coming up. GSGI is comprised of former SEALs and senior law enforcement, both local and federal, so we have an aggregate of thinking and skills that comes from a very experienced background. We're teaching a very unique, very specialized program.

I can tell you right now, teaching military, teaching law enforcement, is not going to make anybody rich. It's going to give you great satisfaction, if that's what you want to do, but it's not going to make you rich. For that, you need to look at the civilian sector, the corporate environment. The personality and leadership building programs, the Outward Bound–type things, they do a great job in building teamwork. And Dick is much better at that than I am. I'd rather focus on the higher-level stuff. A great combination would be: he builds the team and I teach the skills. But I really can't be bothered with the ABCs of building teamwork. I find that to be tedious, while he's very good at that.

• • •

In SpecWar terms, I think the future will be very lucrative. Think about what SpecWar is—a small, precision war concept. From now till probably infinity, the conflicts we're going to see will be very small, very localized, requiring specialized, small units to go in and neutralize the threat. I don't think we'll see major conflict or major divisional warfare, where Army-level deployment is going to be the rule of the day. You'll see Special Operations—highly specialized and sanitary, if you will, very exact in nature. You deploy very high skill levels in minimal quantities, so your risk is minimum and your reward is great.

SpecOps units are flexible, provided you're not overloading their plate. A SpecWar unit is not going to go in there and neutralize two divisions. But a SpecWar unit will go in after a key command-and-control element, and knock it out, do something that can't be done from the air. A SpecWar unit, or several SpecWar units, could go in and eliminate a warlord.

Let's look at Mogadishu. If that operation had been conducted properly, it would have been done with a lot of intelligence up front and with the appropriate number of operators going in to neutralize the threat. They could very well have been successful. That's not what actually happened. They went in with very poor intelligence, and they went in highly announced, with no backup support. That's a result of political leadership as opposed to military leadership.

• • •

I think under SOCOM and JSOC, the SpecOp community—it's not just the Teams now—the SpecOp community is at its best possible configuration with respect to dealing with other military units. Heretofore, Air Force working with Army, Air Force working with Navy, Navy working with Army—it was always catch-as-catch-can. As Desert One proved, and as Grenada proved. But with the formation of the Special Operations Command and Joint Special Operations Command, the leadership is under one hat. Now we have Tier One shooters, one side Army, one side Navy, and support elements—Air Force—all speaking the same language, all training the same way. Which makes for a much more efficient operation, as opposed to showing up for a mission and having turf battles.

• • •

Dick and I continue to work together, and always will work together. We have never softened on our friendship or our natural affinity toward each other. I have a lifelong best friend in Dick, and that friendship cannot be dissolved. That's been proven over and over again.

Mike Purdy
aka Duck Foot Dewey

People join the military for all kinds of reasons. For a lot of kids from crappy backgrounds, military service looks better than any of their other alternatives. That was the case with Mike Purdy. His story is a good example of what someone can accomplish when he's given the right opportunity.

Mike was a young sled dog from the word "go." He was wiry, frisky, and eager to bite the bullet, no matter what caliber it was or who was firing it. I could see that within the first five minutes of his interview for SEAL Team SIX, so I just cut the interview short. Of course, Mike had no idea what was going on, whether he'd just blown it or not. He was just being Mike Purdy.

That's something you need to keep in mind when you're interviewing recruits for a new project, or being interviewed yourself. When I was putting together SIX, I talked to a shitload of guys who looked real good on paper. But I needed people who could think on their feet, who weren't easily intimidated. In the interviews, most of the guys just wanted to give me the "right" answer—tell me what they thought I wanted to hear. I'd sneak out of the interview room and hear the whispers in the waiting room as the guys passed on the type of questions we asked. That's why I did bizarre things or asked dumb-shit questions. I wanted to see who these guys were in person, not on paper. Admiral Rickover did worse things when he interviewed candidates for his nuclear power program. He'd have the candidates sit *on chairs with uneven legs, make them wait in closets before their interviews. At the very least, he always conducted his interviews in stark, uncomfortable surroundings, and he was always cantankerous and unpredictable.*

Mike became one of the young lions with plenty of dedication, motivation, and lots of hunger to accomplish the mission. When he came to SIX, Mike was so new his only language skills came straight from the gutter—no time for language school. Later in his career he became a Philippine cowboy, fluent in Tagalog. He brought no true union skills, but he did have lots of street savvy and an aggressive spirit.

As you'll hear, that aggressive spirit sometimes caused him trouble. He'll tell you about one particular incident, and I want to give you a little background on it. At that time, we'd just had a training accident; Purdy had to put a teammate on a plane out of the site and, ultimately, out of the Teams. This was a serious accident. In Temporary Training Facilities, an FNG stumbled going through the door and let a round go into one of the men. Sure, it was an accident, but it was preventable and it had fatal consequences. After a series of operations, the guy who was wounded finally died.

Naturally, the guys were all a little shook up. I reamed them all new assholes, telling them to pay attention to details and stop dinging rental cars. Everyone was tired, low, and in no mood for any shit. Well, shortly after this, a group of young Air Force officers walking through a parking lot dinged Mike's car. He voiced his concern, which led to a quick "hands-on" dialogue. You'll read about the aftermath from Mike's point of view. Bottom line—I understood

why it happened. I did my best to protect the unit and protect his career. He was one of the shooters worth fighting
for, and I'd do it again today. Loyalty is a two-way street.

Purdy climbed through the ranks, and while he climbed,
he passed along the skills he'd learned. He's doing the same
thing today, teaching op skills to those who have a viable
"need to know." We still see each other every so often, check
each other's pulse to make sure we're both okay. I look forward to the day I visit Las Vegas and see Mike winning at
the big games. He'll bet on just about anything. Of course,
there's nothing wrong with that. He's not betting blind;
he's using his analytical mind to weigh the odds, doing risk
management to weigh what he's willing to lose. Those are
valuable skills. For Mike, gambling is just another training
aid.

NAME: **Mike Purdy**

DOB: **December 15, 1956**

HOMETOWN: **Lynwood, California**

MILITARY: **USS *El Paso*; SEAL Team ONE;**
                       SEAL Team SIX; Defense
                       Language Institute; Red Cell;
                       Dev Group; Naval Special
                       Warfare ONE; SEAL Team
                       FOUR; Dev Group

HIGHEST RANK: **SEAL warrant officer,**
                       designator 7151

SPECIALTY: **Ordnance and weapons**

CURRENT: **Independent consultant**

Some days, I'm kind of surprised that I got to this point. Twenty, twenty-five years ago, when I was driving a candy truck, drug dealer was looking pretty good. That was the career choice that seemed most likely at that point.

• • •

Lynwood is actually part of Los Angeles, near downtown. It's not exactly the best part of town now, and it wasn't great back then. There wasn't organized gang activity but more of a block-by-block thing. If someone else was on your block, they were in trouble. If you were on someone else's block, *you* were in trouble.

I'm the baby of the family; I've got one brother and two sisters. My dad was in the Army for a few years in World War II, then he moved to Los Angeles and went to work for Firestone Tire and Rubber. Worked for them for thirty-six years, until he retired. Not many people do that these days. My mom raised us, and she also worked at this place called Pacific Valves. They were both good people, hardworking people.

I was okay as a student—pretty much straight C average. I didn't exactly apply myself. I just tried to keep my grades high enough to play baseball.

All through high school, I worked at a place called Tom's Candy, which supplied all the candy machines

in Watts. It was an all-right job for a high school kid. I
drove around in one of those step-side trucks, stock-
ing vending machines and all that, and I got to take
the truck home every night. I'd take dates to the
drive-in in that thing. All the candy you could eat.

After I got out of high school, I worked at Tom's
full-time. I didn't really know what I wanted to do,
but after two or three months, I'd decided Tom's
wasn't it. Plus, I just wanted to get out of the neighborhood. I already had a bunch of friends in jail, and a
bunch more heading down that path, so I knew I had
to get out. I went down to talk to an Army recruiter.
He told me they'd give me $2,000 if I came in as a tank
driver. I figured I've been driving this candy truck, so
driving a tank can't be much different. So I said I'd do
it, and the recruiter said, "Great—come down tomorrow and sign the papers."

I went home and told my dad I was going to join
the Army. He just about lost it. Like I said, I knew he'd
been in the Army during World War II, but that was
about it. He never talked about it much—all I knew
was that he'd made sergeant three times, kept getting
busted and making rank back. But when I told him I
was joining the Army, he said no way. He said I'd just
be a ground-pounder, and they wouldn't teach me
any kind of technical skills. We had a Navy recruiter
who lived down the block, and my dad said, "Go talk
to that guy. At least the Navy will actually teach you
something." Little did he know.

First thing the recruiter asked me was, "You want
to be a SEAL?"

I said, "What's that?"

He said, "Ask any Marine who's had his arm broke by one." That was the first time I'd ever heard of the SEALs. I didn't grow up watching frogman movies or anything; hell, I've hardly seen any of them now. But yeah, it sounded good.

So I joined up and went to boot camp, and while I was there I took the screening test for BUD/S. I failed the swim test by about ten seconds. The guy giving the test told me, "Well, you gotta come back." I said, "Shit, in three or four months, whenever I actually have to go through this, I'll *be* ten seconds faster. Why do I have to take the test again?"

He said, "Nope, you got to take it again."

I said, "Well, the hell with this outfit. I don't need you guys." So after boot camp, I went into the fleet.

I was a gunner's mate on the *El Paso*, and I'd been there a few months. One night, I was standing midwatch, which is over at four, and I went to wake up the next guy. Guy named Colvin. I've never seen him again, but I owe him a lot. I get to his rack and I say, "Colvin, get up." He starts hacking and coughing, hacking and coughing—he was a big, fat guy—then he rolls over and goes, "Hey, you got a smoke?" I just looked at him and thought, "God, I got to get off this ship."

So I went and took the screening test again and made sure I passed it this time. I had to finish out a full year on the ship, and then I went BUD/S.

• • •

I was in class number 98. I think about 130 started, and 30 graduated. Right about 30.

I had no idea what I was in for, no preparation. I did the year in the fleet, then took thirty days' leave before I went to BUD/S. I weighed about 195 pounds when I got there, and I couldn't do five flutter kicks. So getting through it was just a matter of hanging on.

But even so, I don't think BUD/S, and especially Hell Week, is something you can really be prepared for. You just have to suck it up and do it. Which was easy for me, because all I had to do to get motivated was look out at one of the ships. I knew if I quit, that was where I was going, back to the fleet, back to big, fat Colvin. So I just made up my mind I wasn't going to quit. They could kick me out, but I wasn't going anywhere on my own.

• • •

The first time I was in combat was Grenada. Four of us left three days before everybody else. Our job was to recon the airfield at Salinas and meet the jumpers. Well, the jump party went bad, we lost some guys on the jump, and the actual recon mission never went off. We got in there and we got spotted by a patrol boat. Long story.

Anyway, after it's all over, turns out everybody else in my boat crew and everybody else in my team was sent to the mansion or the radio station or somewhere, and they'd been in these incredible shootouts. And here I was, picked to go down early and I didn't get to go into any of the heavy action. I was actually kind of bummed.

Panama was different. There was a lot happening,

and we got to do a lot of missions. We were down there for thirty days, doing continuous ops.

Panama demanded the most out of me, and not the way you might think. We were doing just an incredible number of hits, looking for Noriega. Then after he showed up at the Papal Nuncio, we were still going in and hitting his lieutenants' houses, drug dealers' houses, things like that. There were almost always people in the rooms we entered, and having the discrimination not to just shoot—that took a lot. There were a couple of times when we could have popped somebody pretty easy and got away with it. It would've been considered just part of the hazards of war. The actual discipline of *not* shooting—that required a lot of skill.

Don't get me wrong—I'm willing to shoot anybody I need to to get the mission done. But you don't *need* to just go in and kill everybody who moves. That's kind of the easy way out. It takes more skill, more discipline, to get the job done without it.

Experience was part of it. If there'd been a lot of real young guys in the group, I think there would have been a lot more people shot. But I also credit the training we got at SIX, the training the Skipper set up right from the beginning. Training is never going to show you exactly what combat's going to be like. You can't get shot at in training, you can't shoot people in training, so you can't see *exactly* how somebody's going to react to that. But our training was as good as it could possibly have been. As close to the real thing, the physical and mental stress, as it could be.

I said before that my dad was in the Army in World War II—in Normandy, places like that. Like I said, he never talked about it, didn't tell a lot of war stories. Panama went on over Christmas, so after it was over I called home. My dad said, "How was it?" and I said, "Well, to be honest, Dad, they were surrendering pretty fast." And he said, "Huh. Just like the Italians." That's about all he had to say.

● ● ●

I didn't really have much in the way of expectations about the Teams. The Navy was a way out of the ghetto, and the Teams was a way out of the regular Navy. That's how I looked at it, an opportunity to do something better.

But then once you're there, once you make it through, you realize you're part of this family, this incredible family, and nobody can take that away from you. Except for yourself. You've got to hold up your end.

Being part of the Teams—that becomes your ID. Who you are. If you had to face the Lord and you're standing there at the pearly gates, and he says, "Well, what'd you do down there?" I'd say, "I was a SEAL." You have a certain kind of pride when you say it. That pride, that bond between you and the other guys, that can't be duplicated.

We all came from different backgrounds, had different personalities, but that doesn't matter. You become incredibly tight. For the first couple of years, setting up SIX, we were probably gone 320 days out of 365. Just day in, day out, going through the shitty parts of work,

the good parts of work, obviously drinking and partying. You just become brothers.

I have to say drinking was always my favorite operational activity, actually. Shooting came in second.
Not the two at the same time, though.

I never was a big fan of O_2 diving, night compass
swims. It's pitch black, you're just following the compass heading blind, and you're in shitty water and
there's phosphorescence kicking off your fins—you
just feel like this giant lure for whatever's out there.
It's hard work. I never found anything fun about it.

But the worst had to be those high-altitude jumps in
the beginning. Those *sucked*. We didn't have the proper
gloves or anything else, and we were jumping from
thirty thousand feet. It's literally minus fifty degrees up
there. By the time you get to the ground and start thaw-
ing out, you can't move. So you have ten guys on the
ground, half-frozen, all crying like little girls. Some old
Korean woman with a broom could have beaten us all
to death. That was the first time I heard the Skipper say,
"You don't have to like it, you just have to do it."

And that's pretty much how it works. When it's
bad, you just keep on keeping on. You know you'll be
having a beer sooner or later, and you can all laugh
about how bad it sucked. But to be honest, there
wasn't ever much laughing about those first high-altitude jumps. Didn't matter how many beers we had.

• • •

There's one kind of motivation—you're not going
to quit and let your teammates down. That's the motivation that gets you through BUD/S.

Then there's motivation to try to succeed or stand out. As you get older, you kind of lose that. You don't have that motivation to stand out anymore. You don't necessarily want to be the number one frogman in the world. You'll leave that to the next batch of young guys.

Foster Green and I were talking about that the other night. We served together in just about every command. When we were in SEAL Team ONE, we used to say, "They're gonna form up some special outfit and we want to be part of it." So then word went around that there was this new team forming up. Everyone who's interested, put your name on the list for an interview. So myself and Foster, Denny Chalker, all these guys in Echo Platoon at SEAL ONE, we all put our names on the list.

That's the first time I met Dick, when I was interviewing for SIX. I'd heard stories—he was a wild man, he was going to chew your head off. Of course, we're young frogmen then, so we're hearing everybody's Vietnam stories, hearing from the guys who knew Dick on the West Coast. But, actually, working for him didn't mean all that much to me then. I just wanted the command. It wasn't until I actually got there that I realized who he was and what he meant to the place.

So it came my turn for the interview for SIX and I went in. Dick's sitting there, this big guy with this big beard. Quite a presence. He didn't say anything, just sat there. Norm Carley, the XO, was asking the questions. Just the normal questions, what makes you think you'd be a good pick, all that. The Old Man's just sitting there, and right in the middle he goes, "So tell me something!"

I go, "What, sir?"

"Anything, goddamn it! Just tell me something!"

At that time, I liked to do some betting—still do, actually—so I said, "The Raiders in six points are a good bet this week, sir."

He goes, "Get the hell out of here!"

So I leave and I'm thinking, "Well, I sure screwed that up." Next thing I know, I'm getting orders. Either he'd bet on the Raiders and won, or he'd just heard enough.

•   •   •

He was a fantastic Skipper. Once the books came out, people started asking me, "You know Marchinko?" And I go, "Well, I know Marcinko." And then they always ask, "What's he like?" And I always say, "He was the best CO I ever worked for."

It was an incredible time. Things were happening fast, he had a timetable for getting the command ready, the counterterrorism mission was pretty much brand-new. He was just an incredible, gifted leader. He could get you motivated like, I don't know, Vince Lombardi or something.

He gave you the responsibility, he wasn't a micromanager. He expected success. He didn't necessarily tell you how to get it done. He just told you what to get done. That was all. He was results oriented.

The other thing was, you knew that he was *there*. He was there for you, no matter what happened, even if things went to shit. He was always right there with the guys.

Right after SIX formed up, when I was still third class, I got into a fight with this Air Force officer and the guy ended up losing an eye. There were all kinds of charges against me—civilian charges, Navy charges. The Skipper listened to my explanation, took me to captain's mast, and found me innocent. Then the commodore accused the Skipper of whitewashing the whole thing, and *he* took me to commodore's mast.

It would have been easy for the Skipper to cut me loose. It would have been better for him politically. They were trying to hammer him, using this incident to do it. But the Old Man said, "Look, you don't have to put up with this. You can make a big deal, but it's probably better for the command if you don't. Let's just ride it out and see what happens."

He even went up to talk to this guy at the hospital in Bethesda, trying to talk him out of all these charges against me. The Skipper came back and called me into his office. I asked him, "How'd it go?"

He said, "Well, here's what we're gonna do. We're gonna put his other eye out and buy him a dog." That's how far he was behind his guys.

The whole time, the Skipper could have said, "Hey, Purdy, we're gonna let you go." He didn't have to stand by me like that. I was just a young kid, I was nothing. Cannon fodder. I hadn't even worked for Marcinko that long. But he stuck it out with me. After someone does something like that for you, you never forget it. To this day, I'd do anything in the world for him.

And we had that kind of loyalty all through the command. Each team had about thirty or forty guys, and your team chief was God. Bob Shamberger was ours, the driving force. He was like the father of this family. He died in Grenada. Then we'd split off into boat crews, with the senior guys in charge. The junior guys, we used to call them sled dogs. They're at the bottom of the food chain. But it was an incredible family. They're still my best friends, those guys that formed up SIX. Those are my tightest friends. You literally know everything about them and they know everything about you, from your biggest fears to your greatest wishes. And, goddamn, you all put up with each other, still.

● ● ●

These days, I'm an independent contractor, teaching the same kind of stuff we did when I was in SEALs. I work for some private clients, and the government. It's kind of a touchy thing—the people I work for, they want to keep things quiet.

I get to keep doing things I like, and the money's good. Keeps me traveling. I'll probably do this for another four or five years. Ultimately I want to play poker for a living. I have to save up some money and figure out how to end up out there in Nevada. I'll do this as long as I feel I'm still current, still putting out good information.

What I miss is the day-to-day locker room environment. You don't hear new jokes every day, you don't have to be on your toes every day because people are busting your chops, and you're not busting anyone else's chops. You miss that real-world mission, getting pumped up for that. And the access to equipment—planes to jump out of, all the bullets you can shoot, all that stuff. When you're a civilian, you've got to pay for that crap.

• • •

This should be a great time to be in the Teams. It's a target-rich environment out there. I wish this had been our situation in 1980 when we formed up. We were much better suited to go do things without the hierarchy slowing you down and stopping you.

The Teams have gone green—they're controlled by the Army. Now, they fall under Army OPCON, or Joint OPCON, which is another name for Army. So if something comes up, it's no longer like the old days when the fleet commander had a platoon of SEALs and he could make the decision to deploy. Back then, even the JSOC organization was smaller and quicker. Now, even with the regular Teams, it's harder for them to get on the ground and actually do something.

The Teams have gotten bigger and bigger, and more and more top-heavy. The organization is like anything else—as you get bigger, you lose speed and you lose flexibility. You're not as quick as you were, you've got more people watching you, you're spending more money, and you just can't move the way you could before.

And the leadership has changed. I think if Dick were still in there, he'd make a huge difference. One day, years ago, he outlined his vision of where the Teams were going. It was pretty incredible. A damn good plan. Obviously, since he got out it hasn't come to fruition. But more than that, his style of leadership would've made a difference. He wasn't afraid to buck the system. He wasn't worried about making rate. Not all officers are worried about that. There are some very good officers running around in the Teams. But the Teams have admirals now, and that's obviously in some of these guys' minds—"If I don't do anything wrong, I'll get promoted to the next grade." Well, the only sure way not to do anything wrong is not to do anything. That's not how the Teams ought to be run.

• • •

I think there's a great market for the kinds of things Dick has to teach. Everybody could use that, to learn to rely on other people and have other people rely on you. Focus more on the mission instead of yourself— that's the old standard line, starting in BUD/S, "There is no *I* in *Teams*."

Doing what I do, I use the things I learned from Dick all the time. I have to motivate people, instill teamwork. And I learned a lot from Dick—let people do good work, lead from the front, all that.

But, for me, one of the things I remember best about him was his sense of humor. No matter how bad things got, no matter how shitty everything was, he could always find the humor in it. A dark humor, but you have to have that. I use that all the time in the classes I teach.

There are certain people—no matter what's going on in your life, no matter what stage you're in—you hear that person's name or you see them, and it brings a smile to your face. The Skipper's like that for me. He's always cracked me up.

Steven Seigel

aka Indian Jew

When he first started working for me, Steve was one of those clean-cut, all-American boys—mom and apple pie all the way. (We took care of that.) He was a natural athlete, outgoing, always good-natured. Nothing seemed to faze him, and he performed all those crazy SEAL stunts with ease. One of those guys you look at and say, "I'll take more of him."

Reading Steve's interview, you'll see that like so many of these guys, he was a late bloomer. He floundered for a while, needed to face some physical challenges before he could decide what was important to him. His experience, and the experience of so many of these other guys, reinforces something I've always believed. I think it's an excellent idea to spend a hitch in the military before you pursue a college degree. The travel across the country and around the world; the exposure to different situations, different kinds of people; the experience with teamwork and discipline—all of that helps broaden your outlook. You'll get to know yourself, what floats your boat and what you'd eat a yard of shit to stay away from. This observation goes back to the days when I was working at Gussy's luncheonette near the campus of Rutgers College. (The dweeb editor wants me to point out it's now "Rutgers University." Picky bastard.) I'd see the "vet" students—focused, motivated, full of purpose and self-direction. Then there were the "jocks"—having a good time, but basically pissing their lives away. I just hope those jocks got their shit together the way Steve did.

Steve brought with him a belief in teamwork; he always pitched in and pushed as hard to achieve the Team's goals as he did when he was pursuing his personal goals. The Team always took precedence. And Steve was a great guy to have in tight situations. He was a hard-nosed performer, but he could also be a clown. If the pace slowed down, you could count on Steve to break out the levity flag. He'd pull the silliest summer-camp stunts, just to get a laugh—short-sheet bunks, jury-rig another guy's gear, harass anyone at the drop of a K-pot. But Steve never crossed the line into meanness, so the other guys could always laugh with him.

I have to say, I took a certain kind of fatherly interest in Steve's career. I knew he'd make a good officer, and I had fun buying him beers and convincing him that he could make the changes he wanted as an officer. I'd gone through the same thought process years earlier. As an enlisted guy, my supreme goal was to be a chief. That was just about the top, in my eyes. Then I saw how the system worked against the chiefs. It didn't matter how experienced or how operationally skilled they were. Chiefs had to be brutally hard or snake sneaky, or both, just to get their ideas implemented. Real change has to come from the officers. That's the reality.

Another reality—any operational organization has to have a qualified man in the planning/functional area. I've seen officers with minimal time in the field write or approve op plans that might as well come from Pluto, for all the connection they have to reality. (This happens way too often in large joint exercises where the plans are drawn up by part-timers—which is one of the current administration's favorite budget-cutting measures.) The lowliest, greenest, most piss-poor operator could take one look at the plan and see there was no way in hell to get from Point A to Point B, given the terrain within the exercise area. No prob—the planner just slam-dunked it and connected Point A to Point B with Event 3½ Result? The troops got no real training, unless pure, pointless misery counts as training. The command-and-control faction was always selective in addressing the net results of these training exercises. After all, we always won!

I was absolutely determined that this would never happen in any command of mine. I knew I'd need to find ops officers who truly loved operating and had a bone-deep familiarity with it, combined with the analytical and planning skills to translate that knowledge into logistics. Steve started out as a sled dog and worked his way up the chain of command; he knew what was required for proper training, what conditions were needed for the troops to maximize their efforts, and what was the most professional way to pull it all together. There's a lot to be said for "raising your own."

I know Steve will be a key player in moving his new employer into a new market. Fountain Powerboats designs fast boats for racing and, now, for Special Operations for the military and police forces. While he's expanding their access to markets here and abroad, I know Steve will make sure the network of shooters out there gets the kind of support he can provide. Another example of continuing Teamwork.

NAME: **Steven Brian Seigel**

DOB: **September 6, 1951**

HOMETOWN:	Tulsa, Oklahoma
MILITARY:	SEAL Team TWO; Officer Candidate School; UDT 22; SEAL Team SIX; Naval Postgraduate School; SEAL Team SIX; SEAL Team FOUR; Naval Special Warfare Unit 8; Special Boat Unit 26; U.S. Special Operations Command
HIGHEST RANK:	O-5, Commander
SPECIALTY:	Weapons, sub ops
CURRENT:	Director of Defense Operations, Fountain Powerboats

The operations, the training—it all seemed like a hobby to me. When I retired, my wife asked me, "What are you going to do for a hobby now?" People pay a lot of money to do the kinds of things we did on a very routine basis.

● ● ●

My father has been practicing law almost my whole life. With that, he has developed a fairly logical sense of thought; things that fall in or out of that are sometimes black or white—although now that he's seventy-three he's mellowed with that a little bit. But I didn't win too many arguments with him growing up.

Not too long ago, I found out that when I was growing up, my dad always kind of hoped that I'd become a lawyer and go into practice with him. I'm sure that's one of the reasons he was *not* happy when I went into the Navy. But I know he's proud of what I've done since, and that does mean a lot to me.

• • •

My dad came from a large family—eleven brothers and sisters. His father was not an advocate of going on with further education. During World War II, my father was in the Air Force, and that allowed him to entertain the idea of getting a college degree. He did that, and subsequently went to the University of Tulsa law school.

I was never an outstanding student. I made Bs and Cs mostly, a few Ds here and there. Academics was just something you had to do to play sports.

I got a football scholarship to Central Missouri State University, a four-year scholarship that increased each year. My dad thought that was wonderful; it was a gift to go to school, to leave Oklahoma. I treated it as just the opposite. I wasn't mature enough to accept the responsibilities, and within about a year and a half, I was about to fail college. My draft number at that time was three, and I knew I ought to do something before I got drafted. I was taking Army ROTC, and I couldn't seem to show up on time with the right uniform, and that experience pretty much convinced me that I didn't want to join the Army. That's when I looked at enlisting in the Navy.

I'd always been drawn to people, friends of the family and so on, who had served or were still serving on active duty in the armed forces. The stories, the adventure, the travel, all of that always had an appeal to me. But it all fell into place on one visit home, when I was talking to my best friend from high school. He'd joined the Navy right out of school, and he was telling me all these stories about UDT, a bunch of guys who seemed like they ran around the world in wet suits working on submarines. That sounded like a lot of fun. He offered me something that I didn't really know I was looking for, and the timing was right. So I thought about it a little bit, and went right down to the Navy recruiter to find out some more information.

My dad was not pleased. As far as he was concerned, I was throwing away this gift I'd been given. Just wasting this opportunity. At first, he wouldn't even go down to the recruiter with me.

So I went down on my own and told the recruiter what I wanted to do. I said, "I want to join the Navy and go into the Underwater Demolition Team." He said, "Sure, young man. No problem. We'll sign you up right now."

My dad did go down there with me on my next visit and talk to the guy some. But neither one of us knew enough about it to know what the recruiter was really saying, which was, "Sure, buddy—you, like everybody else who joins the Navy, will have the opportunity to volunteer for UDT. You can participate in the screening program. But if you fail any of the screening criteria, then you're going right into the fleet."

That was never anything I considered; it was not in my program, it was not going to happen to me. And it never did happen to me. Of course, it could have happened. It could have been something physical, something medical, something in any part of the testing could have dropped me from consideration. But, like I said, that never happened.

• • •

I never remember being tempted to quit BUD/S. I very much enjoyed the physical nature of it. That's one of the things that drew me to it. I'm sure you've experienced a handful of things in your life and said, "I have a real passion for this." And that's the way it was for me. The training is very, very physical in its nature, and it's one of those things that I very much enjoyed. It *was* hard; you got hurt, you got all sorts of reasons your body's saying, "You ought to quit doing that, it's not wise." But the adrenaline, and the teamwork, being surrounded by other people who are doing the same thing—I can never remember saying, or even thinking, "That's it, I'm going to quit."

The teams are made up of a very diverse group of people. And you'd be amazed at who gets through BUD/S and who doesn't. It doesn't have anything to do with the fact that you're a world-class weightlifter, or you've been a collegiate athlete. That kind of thing helps, but you're going to be out of your environment. You're not running around the track or cross-country—you're running in the surf zone, in deep sand, up in the dunes. The longest runs you'll hit will be anywhere from eighteen to twenty-three miles; you're running in combat boots and long pants, and you and your boat crew are usually carrying a rubber boat on your head, a telephone pole on your shoulders. They put you through different avenues to test your teamwork skills—how do you make it happen, how do you improvise, how do you communicate with one another.

Guys show up built like a spider monkey, very lean and look like they couldn't do ten pull-ups, and they might go through BUD/S a whole lot easier than someone who looks like they could do pull-ups all day long, or run till the sun goes down. Because a lot of those guys get out of their comfort zone—they don't have their track shoes on anymore and they can't stop and tape. Or they're swimming in fifty-degree water without a wet suit, because you have to earn your wet suit. It gets uncomfortable. You swim long enough that when you're pushing fins, your ankles go to sleep and you can't stand up on the beach. But they want you to run up on the beach and knock out another fifty push-ups and go on the next evolution. They don't want to hear anything about your ankles. They want to see if you've got heart. They want to see how you get through it.

That's the neat part about it. That's the bond that any teammate, past or present, has had, anyone who's gone through the training that was started in 1943 and continues on today.

• • •

There are no loners, no lone rangers, when it comes to BUD/S. You finish as a class. I don't know of anybody who says, "Yeah, I graduated that year, but I don't know what happened to the other fifteen guys." It's a very close, tight-knit group, because you work so hard together. If there's a weakness, you pick up for the other guys. You and your boat crew have a rubber boat that becomes integral to your life. You carry that thing everywhere you go, carry it up on your head. Well, not everybody's the same height. You've got short guys and tall guys, and pretty soon the taller guys are bearing all the weight for the craft. So the shorter guys compensate for other things. You pick up on each other's strengths and weaknesses, and you form a unit that is strong overall.

That's become a real trait for the SEAL Teams. They're very tight as a group, big on unity, everybody has fears or weaknesses in some areas, but the more you work together, the tighter you get.

• • •

Combat situations are by nature very chaotic, and we spent a very intense effort in preparing for that. My experiences in combat were mainly in the eight years I was in SEAL Team SIX. Most of those missions were unadvertised—the successful ones, anyway. The unsuccessful ones did get advertised. Someone has to take the blame, or the missions just get too big, grow to a proportion where the media gets involved.

But, whatever the mission, we'd prepare through training. We spent an inordinate amount of time on highly precious skills, and some of those go away from you very quickly. Getting those skills really starts when you go through BUD/S training, laying out the fundamentals of how to plan and execute.

When the balloon went up, you fell back on that training. [In case this op term is new to you—when the balloon goes up, you're committed and there's no turning back.] You worked very closely with your teammates. You not only understood what your role and responsibilities were, but you understood what theirs were, too, and what they would do even if they were out of sight or out of communication. That's what gets you through a combat situation. You can rehearse all you want to, you can have multicontingency plans that you are able to fall back on, but there's always going to be chaos. Your training and your preparation are what get you through that. You have to be able to react to a situation without taking a lot of time to think about it. Maybe it's a live gunfire situation and you're moving people. Or maybe you're in a position to move multiple assets on the water or in the air, and they're all converging together in a specific time line. It's a given that something's going to happen that you don't expect.

It's a focus of the Special Operations community, that high priority on training, and that's what enables you to win the day in most situations. An inordinate amount of skill work goes into it, because you have to have that edge. If you don't, something unex-

pected and catastrophic is going to happen, and that'll
sway how the situation's going to turn.

• • •

I look back on it and there's probably less than half
a dozen people who really had a strong influence on
my direction. Somewhere along the way they saw
something in me that made it worth the effort. Dick
was definitely one of those people.

I first met Marcinko in the early 1970s, when he
was coming back in from overseas, finishing a tour
in Cambodia, I believe. I was a third-class boatswain
mate, E-4 petty officer, when he reported to SEAL
Team TWO and took command as a lieutenant commander.

Oh, he definitely had a reputation. I didn't know
much about it at the time. I was the new guy, only a
year or two at the Teams at that time. This was my
first change of command, and I was looking at how
this change of power occurred. Folks that knew Dick
in the '60s were very excited about him coming back
into the SEAL Teams.

I really didn't get to know him at all, other than he
was my commanding officer, until I decided I was
ready to get out. That's when he stepped in.

What was happening was, I'd been through several
overseas deployments, and I saw no end in sight to
continual retraining of officers. You'd spend a lot of
time with them in the predeployment work-ups and
the fundamentals of working in a SEAL platoon and
eventually you'd go on a deployment together. You
spent about a year with them, you worked with them,

you went on deployment, and then the next time you saw them was when they came back as your operations officer. But their operational time was actually very limited when it came to the scope of things. These prima donnas come back in and think they've been Mr. Operator all their lives, and I just got tired of that attitude. I got tired of having to clean up after them.

That was the one thing that threw me over the edge. I can remember it like it was last week.

In all Navy commands, they have a thing called field day, usually a pretty thorough cleanup. On this one field day, I was assigned to the officers' locker room. I walked in there and I looked in that thing, and it was just trash. It looked like a clothes bomb had gone off. And the contrast to the enlisted locker room—we had the operational gear stenciled and folded and stacked, in a bag, ready to go. There was some organization, some pride. Not like these dirtbags. That's the way I felt about them.

So I'm standing in this mess, and I looked out the window, glanced out there, and I saw three junior officers standing around, with their hands in their pockets, doing nothing. They were making these comments—"I wish these guys would hurry up and get done so we can knock off." I thought, "That's it. I can't pick up after these guys anymore."

So that's when I was entertaining thoughts of getting out and going back to school. I really didn't know what I was going to study; it just seemed like the thing to do. I started making it known what I wanted to do, and that's when Marcinko pulled me aside and said, "Here's some other options for you." He himself was a mustang. This is a former enlisted guy who's come up through the ranks, with a commission, not someone who's just come out of college and gone to OCS or the Academy.

So Marcinko said to me, "Come on over here and let me show you what the other possibilities are." He offered me an opportunity to step out of an operational platoon for about six months and attend night school. At the end of that time period, I'd see if, one, my grades warranted going back to school; and two, if my desire to go back was really genuine. If it was, there were a couple of programs we could look at. If not, I could move back into an operational unit and at least I would know, without getting out and floundering around and then trying to get back in, which was common in those days.

Dick didn't call me into his office for this. When you sat down with Dick it was usually at a bar someplace. He'd make those evaluations—this is a guy who's worth putting some time and effort on, or we ought to just flush him and move on.

I had a trial-and-error period, I had a chance to prove to myself that I really did want to go back to school, and I was willing to treat it like the responsibility that it was. And that was the first time I thought about getting a commission. Up until that time I really hadn't entertained the idea, because officers were something I really didn't have much time for. He said, "Hey, if you really want to do this, they have commission programs, this is how you can qualify for it, this is what we can do."

• • •

I joined the Navy to see the world, have some adventures, and up until the last half dozen years or so, that never changed. In fact, it escalated quite a bit. When we were part of the commission organization and early development of Team SIX, it was never higher. I'd be gone over three hundred days a year, and loving it. It was brand-new, it was high profile, in the way we got our funding, in the way we got permission to do things. There probably won't be another time like that for a while.

There were no rules. We were developing those as we were moving, whether it was tactics or operational security instances or whatever. We didn't have anybody to tell us it was wrong and we didn't have time to sit around and wait for someone to give us their stinking opinion. We just kept moving through it. In a lot of ways, it put us way out in front as far as capability.

Those were some of the items on the "pro" side. The cons—well, we didn't have any time to go back and put out any fires we created. We left a lot of smoldering embers. Some of those things led to command investigations later. Folks who really, really hated the way the command moved—they came back later and used all that as ammunition when they were trying to bury Dick.

We probably could have and should have done it different, but nobody gave us the time to do that. We formed the command; they said, "Outfit yourself"; and we had our first real-world mission just about nine weeks later.

The command was built in those first three or four years. Those were fast-moving years, fast moving and high paced. We had avenues to accomplish things that people join SEAL Team to do. That's what the people who go to Team SIX these days look at and say, "That's what I want to be a part of."

• • •

I certainly enjoyed jumping. We did a lot of unique things with skydiving, and I ended up with quite a number of jumps. It was always an adrenaline rush. We'd be at morning muster by five o'clock, get our safety brief, chute up, and be in an airplane circling over St. Petersburg, Florida, when the sun was just coming up. We'd go out at ten or twelve thousand feet. You're screaming toward the ground at anywhere from 125 to 200 miles an hour. It's a great way to wake up. It's super. There are lots of folks you're jumping with, you're able to fly with somebody and link up, or later on you laugh about who screwed it up. And you come in and you land, feeling energetic about that. And then you go to work. It was always fun to do that.

Back in the early '80s, at Team SIX, we were able to introduce the Ram Air–style parachute. Everybody uses that now. At the time, it was rather unique, and they were only used by people who were involved with jump teams and things like that. Well, we brought 'em in and everybody used 'em. We had to learn how to fly those things. They have a built-in forward air speed, and they're highly maneuverable. We did a lot of unique stuff with that chute, including jumping at very, very high altitudes and opening very high and doing a lot of cross-country work. Flying together as a team and learning how to juggle your weights so everybody can stay together, big guys and light guys alike. All that stuff was unique at the time.

I think the shooting actually became one of my favorite operational functions. That was make-or-break. You could go out and have a bad day and kill somebody, because you're working in such close proximity all the time. You work very, very closely with a shooting partner and/or a team, and everybody had very defined positions to go to, but it was live. We didn't do very many dry runs. One slipup, one "I should have turned left, I should have been right," and you can cause somebody else a great deal of harm. You don't want to lose a teammate in a training exercise. Our first year, there were fewer than ninety people in the whole command, and we probably shot more than the Marine Corps did in their allowance for the year. That's what we needed to do, to get our skills to the level they needed to be. But you don't do that by shooting fifty rounds and then heading home. It's shooting and shooting and shooting, and shooting some more.

•   •   •

I don't know how you motivate yourself sometimes. I don't know if it's stupidity or stubbornness.

Sometimes you have to know when you *should* quit.

The most miserable I can ever recall being was when I was with a swimmer delivery command. If you're either flying the boat or you're navigating the boat, you're busy. You're focused on that, and that's okay. But if you're just sitting there for hours and hours and hours not doing anything—you can get real cold in eighty-degree water after a period of time. Well, on this one trip, I was assigned to go out and stay out for about seven hours. I was supposed to have a certain type of wet suit, it had been ordered, but it hadn't come in yet. So they gave me this thin wet suit and said, "You're only going down to twenty-five feet, you'll be fine." I spent all those hours in about fifty-four-degree water, the wet suit compressed, and I got hypothermia. That was miserable. The whole time, I told myself, "I'm just having a bad night here. I've been cold before."

Then at the end of it, when you're recuperating over a two- or three-day period, you're dehydrated and all the stuff that goes with hypothermia, you realize, "Hey, I probably should have had them come up and got myself out of the boat." It was just a training dive, nothing critical. You look back on it and say, "I should've come up." But no—I was gonna finish the mission.

That was the most miserable, least fun evolution I can remember. All the rest of them—they can be miserable or tiring, but you're with a bunch of other guys who're miserable and tired, too. That's where we end up making ninety percent of our own fun.

• • •

I feel very strongly that leaders have to earn trust and respect. A lot of people who come into the Teams think that their rank should be able to carry the day. That's only there for protocol, as far as I'm concerned. I don't care how senior the guy is—if he hasn't been alongside of you, sweating it out and making that effort, his credibility as a shooter or a planner or someone you can rely on in the trenches is questionable.

Growing up in the SEAL Team, working alongside your peers, that lets everyone get to understand your strengths, understand your weaknesses. They understand your decision tree and they know you're going to make the best decision to accomplish the mission, protect them, and make sure that you inflict the maximum amount of damage on the other guy. That's where you bring it all together.

During my second tour back in Team SIX, I was an operations officer for three years. I was responsible basically for the entire command on a day-to-day basis on a worldwide area. You worked with these guys, you deployed with them, you took care of them when you were back in Virginia and they were on the other side of the world. But most important, when you came together to solve a problem, you were responsible for the overall coordination and planning, the checklist efforts that went by to keep the CO involved. The captain was calling the shots all the time, but he was leaning hard on his operations officer to know every detail.

The hardest thing to deal with in that situation, in

any situation I can remember, was getting the guys back on track when we'd gotten bad news about one of the other units. You had to refocus everybody, get off a temporary lapse. People are thinking, "I wonder what really happened to him. Did we lose somebody, or is it that they just haven't been able to call in?" You have to be able to turn that around and get them back on track, because you could lose other people because they're not focused. That's where the leadership skills come in. I really believe what makes the difference is the respect you earn. You don't show up brand-new to the command and thump your chest to show everyone you're now in charge. You've got to prove yourself, to a certain extent.

The guys understand that and respect it and react to it. That's one of the things that Dick had—the respect of his men. He empowered his team leaders and his people in key positions. And they weren't always the most senior people there. It could be a very squared-away, operationally savvy senior enlisted, or even a junior enlisted, who was best for the job. He was empowered. Everyone else stood out of the way and let that guy do his job.

That's one thing I always tried to do, instill that in new officers in my command. I'd take new junior officers and put them subordinate to a junior petty officer for a period of time. I'd say, "You're going to do what this guy tells you to do. I don't care if it's cleaning weapons, cleaning the boats, squaring away the lines, I don't care what it is. If you've got a problem with it, I want to know." And if he had a problem with it, then he had a problem with me, and we were going to take a hard look at what he thought his contribution could be to that command.

In most cases, that worked out real well. In most cases, the officers came back and told me how much they'd learned. And they learned because they were able to humble themselves and learn from someone who had been there before them. Maybe this guy wasn't as well educated, maybe he didn't look as good, didn't sound quite as polished, but when it came down to operational tactics, he was the teacher and the officer was the student. And that's the way it had to be. That's the way we operated a lot within the SEAL Team. The best person for that job had the strength and everyone else had to fall in line to support that strength. It wasn't, "Let's take an opinion poll," or anything like that. But when it came down to tactical input, people had a very good avenue to participate and contribute. When it came down to, "Okay, this is the way we're going to do it," everybody lined up and we did it.

• • •

The only way to overcome fear is: do it. The last free fall I made, I still had the same butterflies, but by the time I left the airplane, I was so focused on what we were going to do once we left the plane, the fact that I was going to go out of an airplane was pretty far removed.

Some of that stuff never leaves. You're in the water and you realize that you could get vertigo, not know up from down, you're on a rebreather that doesn't emit bubbles, you're in a low-visibility to no-visibility environment, there are things that you can get hung up on and snagged on, all that stuff. You think about that, but then you fall back on just doing the job and trusting your equipment, trusting your training and your skill level. You've got to know that you're the best trained you can possibly be. You've got the best equipment and you're working alongside the best people, so trust it and go with it. Those who hesitate are the ones who can inflict damage on themselves and everyone else. You can analyze something to the point where you never do it.

In the corporate world, I've seen people get tied up in the same avenue. It may not be life threatening, but they just can't introduce themselves to that person, or close the sale, or make a decision. They get locked into a box and they won't let themselves out. I've let that happen to me. I'll say, "This is really stupid. I've done things many times more dangerous than this. The worst thing they can do here is tell me no." But you find yourself hesitating. You have to back up and say, "Why am I doing this?" and reevaluate it, and go ahead and do it. After that, it becomes second nature. Nobody's gonna get killed. You may never see or hear of this person again, they have no impact on your family or your spiritual life, and yet you're hesitating to approach them for some reason. That's ridiculous.

A lot of the things that I was exposed to in my career with the SEAL Teams helped me keep my focus in the corporate world. It gave me a strength, an aggressiveness, you don't often find in civilian life. I find that people very much like to have somebody that they can say, "I want you to establish this, I want you to perform this function," and they never have to check with that person again. So many people need to be led through point A, point B, point C. And it's not even point A, it's A.1, A.2, and so on until you get to point B.

I'm a rookie, I'm only coming up on my fourth month in the corporate world, but already I see weaknesses in people who have been in this world a heck of a lot longer. They go so far and then they stop and wait for directions. Then they go so far again, and then they stop again. That's a heck of an opportunity for me. I'm gonna blow by them pretty quick. And they're always gonna be limited because they've limited themselves. I don't know why. I'm continually surprised.

• • •

Working for Fountain Powerboats is fun. It's fun because it's brand-new. It's kind of like Team SIX all over again. I've been given the opportunity to set up what's called Defense Operations, and there's no limits. The limits are myself. I have a very strong financial backer, a very capable production facility, and I'm working with two individuals with very, very strong name recognition both stateside and abroad. That combination of things allows me to go out and just run. And that's what I'm doing right now.

I'm drawing on what I learned throughout my Navy career, especially during my last billet. Because of my graduate education, the Navy sent me some information and wanted to know if I'd take a look at this area, working in the U.S. Special Operations Command. I understood that this would be a good place to learn the business of where things are going. When it comes right down to it you can have all the finest operators in the world, you can have the best intentions and the most aggressive people, but if you don't have the resources you don't have anything.

This put me in the position of having a direct influence on contracts and moneys to buy and develop equipment for the field. U.S. Special Operations Command was commissioned in the 1980s to be the resource command, own all the money, for the Army/ Navy/Air Force Special Operations worldwide. I was assigned to work within the acquisitions directorate and sent to the schools necessary to give me the correct credentials to become a program manager. I was very much involved in the development of two combatant craft that we currently have fielded in our inventory. It was a lot of boat building, a lot of engineering, using my postgraduate skills, which I had to dust off after all those years. A lot of management, a lot of marketing, a lot of pulling together different levels of field activities for a common project. This was our very first effort to bring something in-house, the hardware in-house in a major procurement force. We were able to do it from the idea, through the funding, to fielding the first two articles in three years. That really was an acceleration in procurement and acquisition. It's used right now as a model for the other services that are trying to get more in line with that.

Owning your own money and having your own acquisition authority is something that the commander in chief at the U.S. Special Operations Command has, and he's the only four-star CINC who has that capability. The other services have to go to other labs or systems commands to have their equipment developed. The reporting chain at U.S. Special Operations Command is very, very short.

We had our own levels of bureaucracy, of course. It's not without fault. If you stay in business long enough, I truly believe you will become what you were designed to overcome. But my replacement is now taking the business of procurement for our community to the next level. A uniform-wearing senior-officer Navy SEAL has a great deal of influence on how money is spent and what it's spent on, to develop the right equipment that's going to be used in the fleet on a short-notice basis.

One of our strengths was we didn't do it in a vacuum. We brought all the users in. All the boat drivers, all the SEALs, everybody who had any influence on how they wanted these things to work and operate— they had a say. It was only as good or as bad as we made it. We couldn't blame it on the contractor.

And that opened an avenue that probably wouldn't have been opened before. I wasn't looking for it, it came to me. It's still gunning up fast boats, chasing bad guys—with law enforcement, Coast Guard, Customs, and military on a worldwide basis. I'm setting up the framework and the baseline for expanding this, educating people to the capabilities, working the congressionals, fielding successful systems. That sums up what I spent over a quarter of a century doing in the military.

• • •

On the corporate side, I feel there's definitely a need for truly good team-building programs. I've been through one of those myself, up in the Washington, D.C., area. Those aren't difficult challenges, especially if you spent a life in the SEAL Teams, but for people who have never had an opportunity to climb something, to work with a group in solving a small problem—I don't care if the problem is nothing but trying to pass someone through a rope maze without touching the ropes.

It can be that simple, but you're working together, talking to one another, helping to form a solution. Most of these problems you could solve yourself pretty easily, but the idea was to work with a team of four to six people. Getting the input, weeding through the good suggestions, the bad suggestions, being diplomatic in saying, "That'll work, that won't work, how can we modify it," making sure everybody had a part to play—all that was very valuable. People walked away from that with a sense of accomplishment. It was like going through a mini-BUD/S for them. They walked away going, "Yes, we did it, we did it together." I look back on it, and that's what people got out of it from a leadership point of view, a teamwork point of view.

It wasn't that the tasks were all that difficult. Some

of it's just swinging on a rope across a creek. If you
don't push off at the right level, if you don't do certain
things, you don't make it. And then you either get in
the water or you get pulled back. I'd look at this and
think, "This is dirt simple." But there were folks
who'd never been put in that kind of situation before.

Some of it's plain old trust. They were being put in
a position where they were going to fall backward
and they had to trust everybody was going to catch
them. It was the fear, one, of being up a little higher
than everybody else, and, two, not looking where
you're going and just trusting that when you fell
backwards, you were going to be caught. There were
a lot of people who had an internal fear of letting
themselves do that. You take a guy from the SEAL
Teams and he wants to do a double gainer off the
thing, do a cannonball into their arms, splatter the
whole group. "Catch this!" But that's what people get
out of it, strength and confidence.

•   •   •

Special Operations in its nature can be very well
utilized because you can get a lot of impact for the
dollar spent. It doesn't take a lot to move us, it doesn't
take a lot to support us once we're there. So from the
operational training and equipment point of view, I
think SpecOps in itself, and I'm talking Army/
Navy/Air Force, are probably as well employed
today as they've ever been. In many cases they're
overly employed, because they're not only in a force-
protection role, they're in police roles, diplomatic
roles. In some cases, you've got people calling the

shots who aren't all that senior, and they're out there working with country teams or the area ambassadors, and helping in some small way provide the input that defines policy. Those things are going well.

The current administration and the administration bureaucracy, those things get worse and worse. Boy, the current administration is something that I couldn't support. But as far as the bureaucracy in the Teams itself, unfortunately it's the natural progression. People get ingrained; they've got jobs, they don't want to lose them, they want to bring in other people. Pretty soon you've got layers whereas before you didn't.

Some of it's accountability. We've had some hard lessons learned in the past. As much as we said those were the good old days, some of those good old things we did are the direct cause of why we have oversight today. You can sit there and say, "Yeah, it's not like it was when I was in." Well, if you'd been a little more mature, there might not be the things in place today. I can look back on it and be just as hard on ourselves, get a little perspective.

But there is a lot of civilian oversight now. Whether it's on Capitol Hill or within the organizations, that can become a layer of bureaucracy or permission or justification that you didn't have before. You've got to weed through this and make sure everybody understands, and you want to say, "They don't *need* to understand. They're the toad in the road that needs to get out of the way. I'm wasting my time trying to get through some of this crap."

Other than that, SpecWar needs to maintain the

flexibility to get around and operate. I think there are going to be more situations where they're going to be called into play, because they're trying to separate themselves from the rest of the services. The rest of the services are trying to become more like Special Operations, because of the economy of force and resources, and competition for those resources. So Special Operations in itself is getting more technical, more and more specialized in areas that will separate themselves from conventional forces. In doing that— well, just be comforted to know there are 125-plus sites worldwide that have Special Operations forces de-ployed that you don't hear about. There are hot spots all over; the world is never at peace.

The bright side of it all is, the equipment has never been better. The stuff they're using now, from the time they enter BUD/S right up to the time they retire, it's always improving. People complain that they haven't got the right bag yet, but I've got to tell you that the bag they're using now is a lot better than it was before. You look at boats, airplanes, the weapons sys-tems deployed with those things—all that has never been better. Never been better funded, never been bet-ter designed, and certainly the resources that are there to make it happen have been very consistent and very high. The training is probably as high as it's ever been.

The force structure is a downfall, in my opinion, for the Teams. I see a degradation we need to turn around. Mostly it's in the officer ranks. We're losing officers in droves, especially junior officers. They're the building blocks for the future. We're going to have a huge gap, trying to fill senior officer positions later.

I wish I had the correct answer. I've only heard bits and pieces of why. There are a lot of dynamics in it. One of the dynamics is there's only one admiral that's in charge of the SEAL Teams East and West Coast and Special Boat Drivers East and West Coast. He's vying for resources and has been given latitude that is fairly narrow—"Here is where your force structure needs to be, here's where your modernization needs to be, and here's the latitude you have to make adjustments." And in many cases the margin is very narrow.

So there's a lot of competition for resources and how you manage resources and how you transfer that into the training and capability of the personnel. As far as the officers are concerned, they're trying to be operational as long as they possibly can, which is good. But they get one tour or so in a SEAL Team and then they go to a staff. I was in the SEAL Teams for twenty-six years and eight months, and Special Operations Command was the only staff job I had.

So I know it can be done. I know things change, but these guys have to find a way to get overseas, where the action is, and diversify themselves in multiple-skill-level areas—whether it be in the swimmer delivery vehicle area, or the combatant craft area—in overseas assignments that are actually in the field. They can't homeport themselves in Virginia Beach or California. Some of that's got to occur now. Some of these guys are very well educated and they have a strong peer group both in and out of the Navy and they see themselves as being limited. They'd love to get in there and do what they wanted to do when they came into the Navy, but what's left for them primarily are staff positions. They see themselves as being able to do that kind of paper pushing quite well on the outside, and get paid a lot more.

Some of it's a cycle thing. I've seen it a couple of times where we're full up in SEAL Teams, and then we're on the road to where manning is so low that you don't know how you're going to meet all your standards. World situations dominate—the economy's good, it's time to get out and do well in other areas; there are other times when the economy's not so good and there's been lots of activity in the military and operational levels are very high. And I'm sure there are other dynamics that are involved with that, too.

• • •

It's all leadership, and it's got to start from the top. It's got to be something that's formed and emulated, and not just from "This guy's a good administrator." He's got to be a well-rounded leader at the top and be able to enforce that and be able to compete with the other services, to define what's good for the SEAL Teams. That's not always a popular position. You've got to be able to articulate that to a commander in chief, whereas before he didn't have to worry about that. You've got to be able to lead from the top, lead from the front. That doesn't mean you have to be the best shooter in the world, the best diver in the world, or any of that stuff. You need to have action out in front, take a positive position, and kick it down the road. And make those adjustments. Your people have to have confidence in you, respect for you, and that doesn't come automatically with rank. Not even by a long shot. I don't care if you're an admiral or you're a leading seaman. The trust is earned.

Dave Tash

aka Cyclops

Cyclops is living proof that the SEAL Team is an equal-opportunity organization—we really do hire the handicapped. I don't think Dave ever had what you could call a normal outlook on life, so modifying his vision really didn't have a lot of impact. He saw things his way and that was good enough. He may have had only one eye, but he had plenty of guts—enough to keep operating and get the insight and experience he needed to focus on making things run better.

In the Teams, Dave had a reputation as a hard worker, someone able to communicate with and motivate the troops. When I hired him for SIX, he didn't have any experience briefing senior officers, but I knew that he'd get lots of practice real fast. If he kept in touch with the troops, he'd be well informed; if he worked long hours, he'd get it all done. And since he wasn't a hot commodity in the Navy, he'd be focused on SIX and his job. Dave never let me down.

Sure, there was a risk in letting him operate with us, but it was a risk we had to take. Otherwise, he'd have no idea what we'd need out in the field. It was his job to get us there, get us back, keep us equipped with the right gear and comms, and plan for the next event. Not an easy task, because we moved around in groups of forty operators or more. Then, in his spare time, he had to budget for all of this and figure out when we were about to go broke, so I could go steal another bag of gold somewhere. Dave did it all, and he did it well.

Bottom line—I went to bat for a guy I knew could do a good job for us. In return, I got absolute loyalty and a real workhorse of an ops officer. The night that Dave creamed in and broke his back was a real Humpty-Dumpty experience—we weren't going to be able to put this guy together again. It was my loss, and the Navy's loss.

About a year ago, Dave brought his class down from Alaska to D.C.; we got together (without the students) in Old Town Alexandria for a modified "Skipper" lunch. It was a real pleasure to see Dave again, and to see him so enthusiastic about his work as a coach, teacher, principal, and mentor. Not something I would have expected from him, but it just goes to show that what the guys from the Teams can accomplish is limited only by their imagination. Cyclops may have limited vision, but he sees more of what's important in this world than most of us.

NAME: Dave Tash

DOB: October 28, 1946

HOMETOWN: Walla Walla, Washington

MILITARY: USS *Chino* (SS341);
                 SEAL Team ONE,
                 UDT 11, SpecBoat Unit 12,
                 SEAL Team SIX

HIGHEST RANK: E-6; lieutenant commander

SPECIALTY: Torpedoman

CURRENT: **School principal and teacher, Alaska**

There was a guy, a SEAL, who went to free-fall school and wound up quitting. I wasn't the only one who looked down on him after that. I don't blame him for being nervous; I was, too. But that's not the point. It was an Army school. He embarrassed the Team. And that's just unacceptable. I had no respect for him whatsoever. I never wanted to be in a situation where I was that person. So, you do what you gotta do.

• • •

We traveled a bit when I was really young, lived in California and Texas, because my dad was in the Air Force—right at the end of World War II, and again in the Korean War.

My uncle was in the Air Force, too, career military. He was somewhat of a hero. The Japanese attacked the Philippines the same time they attacked Pearl Harbor. My uncle was flying a B-17, about to land at Clark AFB, and when he pulled up and went around, the Japanese were coming in. His plane was credited with shooting down the first Japanese aircraft in the war. From there he was part of the campaign in China, and he went on to be a full colonel.

But I can't say he had a big influence on me. Like I said, he was career military, gone all the time, so I didn't spend much time with him. My dad showed me the write-ups of what he did in a couple of books. I mean, it was really neat and I was proud of him, but it wasn't much of a day-to-day influence.

Once my dad got out of the Air Force, when I was about six, we settled in Moscow, Idaho, which is where I finished growing up. Dad did all kinds of things—he owned a store for a while, but mainly he worked with tractors and combines and so on. When he retired, he was the service manager at a John Deere dealership. My mom raised three of us—I've got an older sister and a younger brother—and she's been a bookkeeper since Moby Dick was a minnow.

When I was in high school I played football, full-back and lineback, and I went out for track. Then I also swam on the swim team.

I was pretty much a C-plus student in high school—I wasn't too motivated. I was into sports and chasing girls, which continued right into college. I went to Treasure Valley Community College right after high school, and I majored in football and girls. Then right after that first year was over, I got married, and I went to the University of Idaho the second year.

And I still wasn't too motivated academically. My first year I majored in accounting; I did okay, but I didn't like it much. The second year, I majored in architecture, and I liked it a lot although I didn't do very well. One of the problems was I was working forty hours a week in a gas station while I was going to school. I just didn't have a whole lot of time for homework, and that's hard to do with an architecture major.

Then I heard from one of my neighbors—a lady a couple doors down, who was on the draft board. She said, "Hey, your number's coming up. You're gonna go." And I said, "Wow, I sure don't want to be in the Army." So I joined the Navy.

I didn't have any ideas about being a SEAL. I was really interested in diving. I just figured, "The Navy must have divers. Maybe I can do that."

Then when I was in boot camp—let's just say they weren't real big on information in those days. First thing, they gave us this presentation on submarines, and I said, "Ooh, ooh, that's what I want to do." So I volunteered for that. And then the next presentation we got was on the Teams, and I said, "Ooh, ooh, I really want to do that." These guys seemed like pretty much the ultimate physical kind of guys. I wasn't making it big time in the classroom anyway, everything I'd excelled at in my life had been physical, and so it seemed like the thing to do.

So I tested for SEALs and did pretty well. As a matter of fact the commander told me that out of the group that tested, I was his first choice. But then it turned out I couldn't get orders to BUD/S because I'd already volunteered for submarines. The commander told me, "Well, when you get to your first command, volunteer, and we'll go ahead and accept you."

Turns out they were short of people in submarines, so once they got you in the path, they didn't want to let go. I went to torpedoman's school and told them I wanted to volunteer for BUD/S and they said, "Yeah, yeah, as soon as you're done with torpedoman's school." Then they sent me straight to sub school. Same thing there—"Yeah, yeah, as soon as you're done with sub school." Then they sent me to a subma-rine and said, "Yeah, yeah, once you're qualified."

Well, by this time I had a shot at NESEP, the Navy Enlisted Scientific Education Program. That meant a chance of becoming an officer, so I went to college and studied computer science. I still wasn't the greatest student. You had to keep a 2.5 to stay in NESEP—2.5 to stay alive. So I considered anything over 2.5 a waste of effort. I wasn't after the education, I was after the commission.

When I was done with that, I tried to get into the Teams, and the detailer for NESEP students said, "No, no, we want fleet sailors out of this." But my CO went to bat for me, and as soon as I got out of college and got commissioned, I went to BUD/S. This was almost seven years after I first started trying to get in—seven years of volunteering every chance I could and gener-ally being a real pain in the butt about it.

I was in class 75. I can't remember exactly how many started—sixty-three, sixty-seven, somewhere in there. There were sixteen in the graduating class, but two of them rolled back, so it was fourteen of the orig-inals.

I don't know how many classes can say this, but our class didn't lose anyone in Hell Week. We did have one guy drop the Friday before, because he was scared of Hell Week. The guys that were left got together and had a kind of heart-to-heart talk. We decided if anybody was going to quit, he had to talk to somebody else first.

I don't know if you've heard of SCISM—that's the

military version of the Olympics. All the free world countries would compete in running, swimming, shooting, etc. Virtually everyone from the Navy who went to this SCISM competition would be from a SEAL Team, or the Teams—UDT wasn't around then. My buddy Bob Baird was the Navy pentathlon champ at the SCISM competition three years in a row. Nobody else in BUD/S could even begin to keep up with him in swimming, so I was his swim buddy going through training.

Tuesday night of Hell Week, we got our first break to sleep. I was sitting on the edge of my rack with tears running down my face and Bob said, "What's the problem?" And I said, "I can't do this." Bob just said, "All we have to do now is sleep. So why don't you sleep and then you can quit when you wake up." Well, I never thought about that. So I got into some dry clothes and we slept for about an hour, and then they got us up. I didn't feel like quitting again for the rest of the week.

Then at some point, Bob says, "Jeez, I don't think I can make this." I just say, "Bob, shut the fuck up. Everybody's suffering. This is hard for everybody, it's easy for you, I don't want to listen to this bullshit anymore, just swim." At the end of Hell Week he said, "Gee, thanks. I really appreciate what you said that time." I said, "You were serious?" He said, "Hell, yeah, I was serious." I didn't have any idea. Not that I would've said anything different if I'd known.

I cannot imagine a class of one making it through

Hell Week. You can't stay up all the time, mentally up, mentally tough every second. You need those other guys to bail you out. There was one guy whose knee got so bad he couldn't walk, so we carried him. That's what makes the Teams what they are. They make you depend on other people.

• • •

The guys I deployed with in SEAL Team ONE, there were two officers and twelve enlisted. We got real tight as a platoon. Once we were up in San Francisco on some training exercises. The platoon commander said, "Okay, liberty's down. You know you need to be back tomorrow morning at such and such a time." The guys just sat there, and he said, "What's up?" And we all said, "We thought we'd go someplace together." And we did. This isn't normal in the military, but it's pretty common in the Teams. You're not supposed to fraternize with officers and all that crap, but that's not the way it is in the Teams. I drank with my guys and ate with my guys and we partied together and we did everything together.

I only had one guy who had a problem with calling me "sir" when we were working and "Dave" when we were drinking beer. Finally I said to him, "You keep calling me 'Dave' while we're at work, so I'm going to make it real easy for you—you call me 'sir' all the time." But everybody else could handle it. I could be Dave their buddy, and they could come to my house and I'd go to their house, but when we were working, I was the boss.

• • •

You learn a lot of motivation in BUD/S. There was a point when we were rappelling, and that pretty much scared hell out of me. But my attitude was, "I've come this far—there's no way I'm gonna bail out now. If this kills me, it kills me. They're gonna *have* to kill me to get me out of here." Then after BUD/S it becomes a frame of mind. Fear can work both ways. It can stop you from doing something, or it can force you to do something. What it comes down to is, there are no options. You're part of the Team, it's part of the job.

•   •   •

One night, when I was at Unit 12, the ops officer there, I was having a party at my house. I had a recurve bow hanging on my wall. My CO saw it and he said, "Oh, you shoot a bow?" I said, "Yeah," and took it down and strung it up and plunked on the string a couple of times—just bullshitting around. Then I went to unstring it. I had my foot on one end and my hand on the other, pulling on the middle of the bow to relax the string. When I moved the string around so it'd come off, one end of the bow slipped and sprung up and hit me in the eye. Presto—just like that I was blind in that eye.

For a while, it looked like I was going to have to leave SEALs. The Special Warfare commodore, the CO, my past COs, they all went to bat for me. But BuMed makes a recommendation to BuPers, and BuPers does their thing. They could probably buck BuMed's decision, but they don't. There was this commander at BuPers who was just an asshole. He said,

"This isn't going to happen. If you're a SEAL, you're a combat swimmer. What if you're out swimming some night and there's problems and you're hit with a piece of shrapnel in the right eye and you don't have a left one?"

"Well, what if I get hit in the left eye?"

"That's not the point."

"Look, if I get hit with a piece of shrapnel, it's probably going to go on through to my brain and I'll probably die. And if it doesn't kill me and I die because I'm blind, I don't know why that should bother you. It isn't going to bother me."

But he just said, "Nope, it isn't going to happen."

The detailer at the time was a friend of mine. He said, "Well, I can't move you without approval from BuPers, but I can keep you at this command forever. So we'll just keep you here until this jerk at BuPers moves on and we'll try it again with the next guy."

So while this is going on, Marcinko comes along. He'd fired his ops officer for SEAL Team SIX and he was looking for another one, and my name came up.

In the interview, I said, "Well, I've got this problem because of my eye."

And he said, "I'm real fucking busy. Do you want this job or not?"

I said, "Yes, sir, I do."

Afterward, I called the detailer up and said, "Can Marcinko really do that? Just kind of ignore this situation I'm having?" The detailer said, "Yeah, he can have anyone he wants. If he wants you, you're in. Congratulations."

So I moved to SIX as ops officer. Everybody wanted to get into SIX, and hell, I'm having trouble staying in Special Warfare. Then Marcinko took me in, and that was the end of it. I put on civilian clothes, grew long hair, and was blessed.

● ● ●

One of the questions Dick asked in the interview was, "If I told you to, would you tell an admiral to get fucked?"

Silly me—I took that question to mean, "Would you be loyal to me?" You know, kind of a hypothetical way of asking the question.

And so I said, "Sure, if that's what you want. You're the boss." I had no idea that he was going to afford me many opportunities to do exactly that—tell an admiral to get fucked, in just those words. This wasn't some hypothetical, abstract question.

Dick was a very flamboyant character. Still is. I drank lunch with him about a year ago and he hasn't changed a hell of a lot. But we alienated ourselves from the rest of the Teams quite a bit. I'm not sure I would have done that in his situation, but hey, it doesn't matter if I agree or disagree—he's the boss. I was, and am, real loyal to him.

I'll tell you the kind of boss he was. When I got to SIX, I'd already been an ops officer, and I knew how to play that. Messages come in and I draft a response and take it to the XO. The XO chops it and gives it back, and I take it to the CO and he changes whatever he wants and signs it and releases it.

Well, I'd been at the Team for I think three days, and

I took a message in to the XO and he just kind
of ignored it and handed it back. So I walked it
over to Dick, the CO, and he said, "Didn't I give you
message-releasing authority?"

"Yes, sir."

"Well, release the message."

"Don't you want to read it first?"

"I'll read it when it's on the board."

So I was releasing messages he hadn't even looked
at.

After a couple of weeks of this, I went in and I said,
"Sir, do you think we can talk?"

"Sure. What?"

"Well, I'm writing a lot of messages that have to do
with policies of the Team. So maybe we should talk so
I can get a feel for exactly what you want, so when I
write these messages, I'm doing it along the lines of
what you want."

He just looked at me and said, "Write the messages
the way you think they ought to be written. If I don't
like them, I'll fire you and hire someone else."

It was basically, "I ain't gonna school you on shit. I
don't have *time* to school you. I hired you because I
think you can do it, and if you can't do it, I'll get rid of
you."

The idea that I had his backing, that he had that
much faith in me, it was quite a compliment. The idea
that I could just go out and do what I think I ought to
do, and if it's not right, I'll die later—well, it was a little bit intimidating, too.

One time I wrote a message to JSOC and told them

we were going to stop training. They were supposed to give us a certain amount of money and they hadn't come through. Now, that money was spent, I'd already spent a bunch on airplanes. All of a sudden I hear we're not going to get this money at all. Marcinko's out of town, so on my own, I sent a message to JSOC and said we're going to quit training.

They called on the phone and said, "What the fuck are you talking about? You're not going to quit training."

I said, "I know, but I need to do it this way because I need for SURFLANT to give in." *[SURFLANT is the military acronym for Surface Force Atlantic.]*

JSOC says, "Well, you can play any games you want. Just don't stop training."

"No sir, we won't."

That was Friday night. Saturday morning I got a phone call from the SpecWar rep at SURFLANT— "Okay, you got the money."

Marcinko showed up the next week, looked at the message board, and said, "What's all this bullshit about?" I told him what I'd done and why, and that it worked, and it was fine by him. We didn't have a major discussion about it. Not even a minor discussion. Any other CO I'd ever had would've gone apeshit that I'd done this on my own authority. Not Marcinko.

I don't know what more you can ask out of a boss. He expected you to do a good job, he gave you the freedom to do it and the backing to do it. I've had bosses before who said, "I want you to do this task—

no, no, not that way, *this* way." I've said to people before, "You're real competent—I'm sure if I do it this way, it'll work. I'm real competent, too. I'll get it done *my* way."

That never came up with Marcinko. He watched everything I did, but he didn't interfere. If things weren't working, he'd call you in and say, "Things are not working. Fix 'em." I never got that speech, so I don't know if he said, "Try this, try that." But he definitely called people in and they'd try it again. But I tell you what—they weren't going to try forever. You're screwing up, you've got the word you need to make things work, and that's all you're going to get. SEAL Team is not an organization of excuses, and working for Marcinko was definitely not that way. As long as you were producing results, life was fine. If you stopped producing, your life got real shitty, real fast.

• • •

I'd been at SIX for a while, about a year and a half I guess, and Blue Team was doing quite well. Gold Team, which started out with most of the experience, wasn't doing so well. They'd changed team leaders several times, and Gold Team still wasn't coming together the way Marcinko wanted. So he asked me if I wanted to be the team leader. Technically, it was a demotion, but it was a chance to operate again, so damn right.

Well, that was a big controversy. The XO, Norm Carley, was upset about it. He said, "What are you going to do when you go in a room and you can't see everything on the left?" I said, "Well, it's pretty straightforward. I'll go to the right and the next guy'll go to the left."

Anyway, Norm didn't have to worry about it. I never got to be team leader because I broke my back.

That wasn't a very good night. I'd gone down to New Mexico, jumping squares and getting some practice doing HAHO. I've got to confess, I always hated jumping. If you're diving and everything goes to shit, all you got to do is get to the surface and you're okay. But if you're in the air and everything goes to shit, when you get to the surface you've got big problems.

Well, this was going to be my last jump before I headed back to Virginia. I went out and opened, and I had two cells on the right side that didn't open all the way. I messed around with them a little bit, and one of them opened, one of them didn't. So now it's decision time. Do you keep the three hundred bucks or do you see what's behind door number two? This chute was holding me in the air, my reserve was also a square, and I didn't have an abundance of confidence in squares anyway. I sure as hell didn't want to dump my main, pull my reserve, and see what it looked like, knowing that was it, no matter what it looked like. So I decided to keep what I got. Well, that meant to go straight, I had to keep one steering toggle higher than the other.

So I got near the ground, made a circle, figured out which way was into the wind, where I was going to land, all this. Well, just as you come in and land, you flare the chute out, pull down on the toggles, and take all the forward speed off the chute. Well, I was a little preoccupied with what I was going to land on and things like that, and I ended up pulling these steering toggles down even. Which put me in a spin and threw me out parallel to the ground, right at the ground.

I hit pretty hard. Shattered my elbow and broke my back. My first concern was being dragged by the chute. So I got the chute off and lay down and hoped I'd get better. I lay there for an hour, hour and a half, until it started getting light. And I'm not getting any better.

Meanwhile, a plane's circling, and I knew it was working its way over to me, looking for me. I was in a foot and a half of brush, wearing a camouflage suit. I knew there wasn't much chance they were going to see me. I didn't have a flare with me, don't know why. That was probably the only jump I ever went on I didn't have a flare with me. Well, our chutes were light blue. So I got up and spread my chute over some bushes where it could be seen. The plane circled a couple of times over me and took off, so I figured they had me. I knew my guys would come and find me. And they did.

I spent a few days being shipped around from hospital to hospital, trying to get back to the East Coast. There was a lot of stuff going on at SIX, so the whole time I talked to the guys several times a day.

Finally, I just said, "I'm checking out. You guys aren't doing anything for me that I can't do for myself at home." I made up some bullshit story about needing to get home because people were bothering my wife and family, something like that—it was a lie, so I can't remember. I went to work the next day.

Every now and then I had to stop and lie down on the floor, but there was a lot going on. I had a lot to do, so I went and did it.

• • •

That was it for the Navy. A one-eyed guy with a broken back—they weren't gonna go for it.

So I got out of the Teams, and got involved in some businesses back in Idaho. And among other things, I started coaching football for a high school in Genesee, Idaho. I decided I liked that a lot, and I wanted to be a head coach because the head coach I was working for was an idiot. So I went back to school and got another degree. The state of Idaho wouldn't let me get a teaching certificate with a computer science degree, I don't know why. I was pretty close in math, so I got a math degree and teaching credentials. This time, by the way, I had about a 3.9 average. It was just a matter of priorities.

Before that, teaching never crossed my mind. Whenever I go to a reunion and people ask what I'm doing and I tell them I'm teaching, they just break up laughing. A couple years ago, an old friend called me up and said, "So I hear you're teaching." I said, "That's right." He said, "Yeah, that's what people are saying. Come on, what are you *really* doing up there?"

I came up to Alaska because in the state of Idaho, garbagemen make more than teachers. My disability would have been more than my paycheck. There's something wrong with this picture.

• • •

One thing I took away from the Teams was the idea of being the best. I have very high expectations of my students. I motivate them, get them to push themselves. Having been a SEAL, that means a lot to kids. If they think their teacher used to be a hotshit SEAL instead of a nerd, that's pretty cool.

This summer, I'm tutoring a kid who's going to be a freshman. He's new, and he looked at the other kids who've been with me awhile and he said, "They're way ahead. Can I get way ahead?" I said, "Well, we're kind of behind the eight ball here, but let's see what we can do."

So we got through pre-algebra and algebra I when he was in eighth grade, with him doing two and three lessons a day. Now he's working on algebra II, at two lessons a day through the summer. His objective is to finish up algebra II, statistics, geometry, and trig in the next two years, so he can take calculus his junior year.

It's just real easy to motivate kids. I like working with kids. It's the teachers who give me problems—I think they're a pretty sad lot. When I was in the Teams, the mission was number one. The Team was number two. You got the mission done, and it didn't matter if you died doing it. But you also took care of the Team. You—your own self-interest—that came in third.

But my experience with the teachers here, their number one concern is themselves. The mission is teaching the kids, and that's number three. They worry about themselves, then the other teachers in the union, then the kids. I don't have a lot of friends who are teachers. I don't like that way of thinking.

I guess I'm kind of resentful of the civilian attitude in general. That's why I think CrossRoads, what Dick's talking about setting up, is a great idea. Before you can really become part of a team, you have to know yourself real well. And there's no better way to do that than with an intense physical experience. I've seen a lot of places that try to do that, and the people in charge don't know their butt from first base. Why not have someone who knows what they're doing set it up?

• • •

But like I said, kids are pretty easy to motivate. I have this PT thing I do with them that's pretty challenging. A bunch of us sat down and did a thousand sit-ups together. It sounds like it's a real hard thing to do, but it's not. If you work up to it, your body gets so it doesn't mind.

I've got a kid right now, last year was his first year with me. He's got shit for a home life, and I think he probably ought to be in jail. Well, this kid got involved in the PT and he realized, "Hey, I can get in pretty good shape." Then he started talking about going into the Army and maybe being in Special Forces. I told him, "Why don't you go for SEAL Team? Why settle for second string?"

He said, "Well, I just wasn't sure if I could do that." I said, "Sure you can. You don't have to do it tomorrow. We've got some time to get you ready." So that's what we're doing. Now he's got some motivation, and some focus.

There's one family I taught, and the oldest kid, a girl, started doing PTs with me. She went into the Naval Academy, and she told me that when she got there, the plebe summer thing was pretty much a joke. She was ready for it. She's in the fleet now, and one brother is in his junior year at the Naval Academy, and the youngest brother starts there this summer.

Another kid wants to go to the Academy and become a SEAL. We've talked about it and I've told him, "The Teams aren't football teams or basketball teams. You don't get in real good shape and go play Teams. You have to be in real good shape to do the things asked of you, but it's not an athletic event. The Team refers to teamwork among the people, but this ain't no game."

Looking back on my time in the Teams, it's the most important aspect of my life, the most important thing I've ever done. It's had the most effect on my life. I've held it out as an aspiration to a couple of kids, and I'm helping them get there.

Albert Tremblay
aka Doc Tremblay

Al is from the old school; he is thorough and demanding. But no matter how hard he is on other people, he's even harder on himself.

As you'll find out, he's another one of those bad students who done good. He didn't exactly excel academically in his youth, but he's always been a fanatical learner. He reads God knows how many publications every day, just to keep up with current events, breakthroughs in medicine, developments in weaponry, and changes in whatever else he's interested in. Al is precise and skilled in everything he does—cooking, restoring weapons, building model ships, bandaging a chewed-up arm. Once he decides he's going to take on a project, he saturates himself with knowledge of the topic, and then systematically attacks the mission. Do not try to talk to Al when he's in this mode. No response, except maybe "Shut the fuck up, I'm busy."

And do not ask Doc a question unless you have time to hear the complete answer, the reasons why it's the correct answer, and all the other answers he considered and rejected. That's what you're going to get, like it or not. (That's one of the reasons we call his wife "Saint Donna.") Al's other sin is his shopping addiction. When we went overseas, we always allocated extra cargo space just for Al. We knew that while he was out greasing hands and working the grass roots, he was also sniffing out bargains, whether he needed another hand-forged toenail picker or not. Al's greatest challenge, to date, was becoming com-

puter literate. He fought that tooth and nail, and it still takes a few Bombays for him to admit that it works and he can work it.

Professionally, Al knew how to make the medical system work. When he became a command master chief, he figured out how to make the process better. Unfortunately, Al was at the bar with me and lots of the other guys when patience was being handed out. Doc has a very low tolerance for incompetence in any area. He is well diversified and highly skilled in everything he does; he doesn't understand why everyone isn't the same goddamn way.

There's something I've noticed about Al and other corpsmen in combat. Their primary job is to save lives; that skill also makes them very good at taking lives. Sort of a human "reverse engineering." If they can fix it, they can break it— hard and fast. They appreciate action, discipline, clear leadership. People trained to make life-and-death decisions in the field do not appreciate bureaucratic bullshit. They're doers, and they want to do things with a purpose and sound reasoning. Anyone who served with Al Tremblay got a good dose of that medicine.

Al and Donna are both retired corpsmen these days, both great cooks, both very talented. They look out for young sailors who show promise, and they stay in touch with professional friends they've developed. These days, Al is even making a serious effort to overlook some of the "sins" of you civilians. It's not easy, but he's trying.

NAME: **Albert J. Tremblay**

DOB: **July 10, 1943**

HOMETOWN: Cambridge, Massachusetts

MILITARY: Corpsman; Navy Underwater Swim School; classified underwater recovery project; Navy parachute jump school; Marine recon battalion; Explosive Ordnance Disposal (EOD) locker/ station hospital, Newfoundland, Canada; Guantanamo Bay, Cuba, hospital/ diving locker; Quonset Point, station hospital/diving locker; Southeast Asia (Laos); Central/South America; Middle East; BuPers; SEAL Team SIX (OpNav 06-Delta and Red Cell); Command Master Chief, Naval Medical Research and Development Command

HIGHEST RANK: E-9, master chief

SPECIALTY: Medical corpsman, combat swimmer, Naval parachutist

CURRENT: Retired; gunsmith and "otherwise doing whatever the hell I want"

I really don't remember anything warm, fuzzy, fond about my family. They're past history. As far as I'm concerned, they don't exist, and as far as they're concerned, I don't exist.

In the summers, I couldn't get up to Vermont fast enough. I used to go up there with a family friend. We worked in small logging camps, a small cattle ranch up there—worked and played outdoors, just got the hell out of Cambridge.

At home, I preferred to be down in the basement tinkering with old junk. Back then, it was okay to go and buy a gun, tear it apart, and play with it. Bob Landseer, a friend of my father's who was in the Army in World War II, really helped me a lot with learning what I wanted to know about guns—why do they shoot, how do you make them shoot. So I used to go out and buy gun magazines whenever I could. I did other stuff—I built wooden models of ships, plank on frame, the old-fashioned way. Still do that today.

• • •

I sucked in academics. I did what I had to do, but there were times I never thought I'd get out. I threw myself into math as much as I could, took four years of Latin. It was an escape mechanism for me. The only club I was a member of was the Order of Demolay—went as high as scribe. I guess that means I was one of Dick's favorite pencil-dick pencil-pushers.

I did better in sports. I ran track, was on the tennis and swimming teams. I'm trying to remember back—I know I lettered in swimming and tennis, I may have lettered in track. I honestly don't remember. Man, it's hell when you get old. I know I made the regional championships for two years.

My senior year, a recruiter came around to the high school, and I just picked up a bunch of literature—Army, Marine Corps, Navy. I tried to go in the Marine Corps but then they found out my father and mother were legally married, so I wasn't eligible. That's a Navy joke.

Actually, the Navy was always my first choice. They offered a lot of educational opportunities, and that was one thing that really sparked my interest. I really wanted to be a gunner's mate. Back then, they had a special accelerated advancement pay program—if you had certain skills, you could go into an accelerated pay grade. I could've gone in as a recruit, finished boot camp, come back as a second- or third-class gunner's mate.

But I was seventeen when I signed up, so I had to have my parents' signature. They wouldn't sign the papers unless I agreed to do something medical. I don't know what they were thinking, don't really give a shit, either. I just said, "Fine, sign the fucking papers." So they did and I did, and that's how I got to be a corpsman.

• • •

I didn't plan on going into UDT/SEALs—I didn't even know who they were, what they were.

I did a couple of tours as a corpsman with the Marines, and in 1963, I went down with them to Cuba. The Navy paid for my SCUBA qualification courses, then I went to the Navy Underwater Swim School. After that six-week course I went back to Cuba and worked part-time at the hospital and part-time at the diving locker. That was where I really first had exposure to UDT/SEALs, and it sounded pretty interesting.

Then, in 1964, I went to deep-sea diving school— part of heading for UDT/SEALs. There were nine of us altogether. Halfway through I said, "What the fuck does this have to do with UDT/SEAL Team?" Nobody could give us a good answer, why we had to be deep-sea diving medical technicians to go to UDT and SEAL Team. So we said, "Fuck you, we're outta here." If I knew then what I know now, I probably would have said, "Oh, I see where it's going." But I didn't want to be a deep-sea diver, and nobody could ever explain it to me then.

I had swim quals and SCUBA quals, so after I told them what to do with their deep-sea diving course, I ended up going aboard an AKA, an amphibious troop transport. This was in 1965. They had a classified underwater recovery project, and they put me right into that project, working with Special Warfare. That's when I first met Dick. He was on the USS *Rushmore*, and we weren't working together, but the project that I was on involved contact with him because of the UDT he was with.

We were both second-class petty officers, E-5, at the time. I said, "We're gonna meet up later on," and he said, "Fucking right." And we did. Of course, that took a few years.

• • •

Well, by 1965, I'd decided that I definitely wanted UDT. Going with the Special Warfare community, I knew I'd work with people who deeply understood a commitment to responsibility. People who were willing to work not only harder but *smarter* to accomplish goals—mission goals and personal goals. You take that camaraderie, and you find your own abilities being honed to a fine edge. You know you can actually accomplish things, not only on your own but also by working with people who have the same ideals you do.

Look at the word *team*, okay? No matter how I look at it, there's no *I* in the word *team*. I don't remember who said this—if you break the word *team* down, it means "Together Everybody Achieves More." It works. And it works that way because you actually believe it can be done, and you're given leaders who say, "Yes, it can be done," and you're allowed to do it.

That's why I was so determined to get to UDT/SEALs for all those years.

• • •

I did that classified project on the AKA for a year, and then because I was also a clinical lab tech, I ended up getting orders for shore duty. I wasn't real happy about that. But I took the orders, down at Quonset Point, and I was also there as the diving corpsman for the chamber operations.

I kept trying to go to UDT, UDT, UDT. And they kept saying no, no, no. So after Quonset Point, I ended up getting the Explosive Ordnance Disposal locker and dive locker up in Newfoundland. I was there three years.

From there, I got picked up to go to the very first class as medical services technician, which was advanced independent duty, plus medical admin—both combined. I had orders with the late John Christie, an old friend. We were both going to either UDT 21 or SEAL Team TWO. I said, "Oh man, this is outstanding."

John went to SEAL Team TWO and I went to the Bureau. They sent me to the Bureau of Naval Personnel as a detailer for the Special Warfare community and the submarine corpsmen. So I'm sending other people where I wanted to send myself.

At least I could write my own orders, which I did after a year and ten days. That was a year and nine days too goddamn long, as far as I was concerned, working with a bunch of bureaucrats. But I was able to help the corpsmen in the Special Warfare community and the submarine community a whole lot, and made a lot of good connections through that.

Now it's 1973. I went to deep-sea diving school again, and I blew the left side of my face—a compression fracture and a sinus bleed. This happened on a dive, a big major squeeze. But I kept on going, finally passed out, in the pot.

They told me, "You're out of here and out of the Navy." I said, "No, I'm not." I was offered two choices. I could either go ahead and drop—"Don't worry about it, go on to your next billet." Or I could take a med board and then have a *lot* of problems. I said, "I ain't taking a med board. No way."

So I went ahead, took another ship, had a tour of duty up in New Hampshire, then got sent back down to Norfolk. Now, I still haven't given up on UDT. In 1979, when I was down in Norfolk, I called SpecWar Group TWO and talked to the master chief over there. He said, "Hey Al, call so-and-so, and tell him to talk to me and let's get it done. Let's get you over here."

So I called the training officer of this team that had a billet for an E-8 corpsman. I told him, "The only thing I need is a refresher dive and a couple of ref jumps. I'm gonna be a little slow, but I can do the job."

He said, "How old are you now?"

"I'm thirty-six."

"You're too old, and we don't have the time or the money to send anyone to refresher training. Thanks very much for calling us." And the son of a bitch actually hung up on me.

So I called back and he said, "Well, Senior Chief, you're too much of a risk because of your age," etc., etc., ad fucking nauseam. So I hung up on *him*.

I talked to Dick about it, and he said, "Don't worry about it. This is what's coming down the road. Finish out your tour here and your tour there, don't ask any questions. Just take a set of orders, oh, around 1980. We're putting SEAL Team SIX together. For right now, I want you to go to D.C."

So I went to D.C., and that's when he picked me up for SEAL Team. That's when we were putting together OpNav 06 D and Red Cell.

Then he buried me for three years, because something else was coming on-line. "Welcome and goodbye. This is what I need you to do, this is where I need you, this is why I need you." He was very selective in who he singled out for this thing coming down the line in 1984. And there was a purpose why he wanted me up in D.C. and I saw the purpose, and I didn't question it.

• • •

One of the biggest reasons why Dick wanted me up there is because we were going to need some good medical support. We all have long hair, big mustaches, a couple of guys have beards. Walk into a military treatment facility and show an ID card, and we'd hear, "Well, you people are out of uniform," blah blah blah. They had to be massaged in such a way that when we showed up, there'd be no questions asked. Well, I just happened to be there at Bethesda, and I developed a medical setup for us there that was never questioned.

I had a commander there who was internal medicine and a chief warrant officer as his assistant. I screened them out, talked to Dick about them, Dick talked to them. And they were on call for us, us and our families, twenty-four fucking hours a day.

There were any number of times when Dick would say something like, "Hey, did Denny call you?"

"No, he didn't."

"Give him a call, Kitty's sick."

I'd call Denny and say, "I'll meet you over at the emergency room." This is with Kitty's first pregnancy and she's feeling a little sick. The commander was there. No questions asked.

Once we were out at a training site and one of the guys got bit by a brown recluse spider. We couldn't get him out for a couple of days. When we got him over to Bethesda, he was in, under surgery, isolated, taken care of immediately. No questions asked.

It was kind of unique for the people at the clinic and the hospital to have these secret superdark guys coming in there. They kept us in a very high-light, high-security area, because it made them feel good about *themselves*, doing something with these secret people. An ego stroke for them. So you give them the ego strokes, you allow them to be involved, make them a part of the Team in some sense. They couldn't go out in the field with us, they couldn't know what we were doing, but we never talked down to them, always appreciated what they did for us.

Dick knew that we had to have that resource available. He put it on my shoulders, and I took care of it. He sent me up there a year and a half in advance with that in mind.

• • •

It all comes down to trust and loyalty. Dick and I have known each other and been together off and on since 1965. I trust him, and the word *trust* is something I take very seriously. I don't trust very goddamn many people, but I trust Dick. And it works both ways.

Dick was an officer, and I was enlisted, but he trusted the senior enlisted decisions. He trusted our capabilities. He held you accountable. If you fucked up, he wanted to know why. He'd help you rework it, help you learn from your mistakes. He was one of the very few leaders I had who wanted to know, *why* don't you understand, *why* don't you know. And you tell him why, and he'll work it out with you.

He'd say, "Okay, this is an exercise problem. This is a real mission problem."

"Question, sir"—that's spelled with a *c* and a *u*. "I'm not clear on this, and what are my resources?"

And he'd say, "Okay, asshole, these are your resources, and this is what it means." He'd break it down for you and make sure you understood it. Never, ever, never would he cast aspersions on you if you asked a question. If you *didn't* ask a question, he'd get pissed, because that's when you're going to fuck up.

And then there's loyalty. Most of the guys can tell you about some time Dick stood up for them. For me, he was willing to take me back on board and take a chance on me, at a time when other people wouldn't. Of course, it wasn't a charity case. He knew I had shooting skills he needed, and other skills. This was one of the things Dick would do—he would recognize and capitalize on your individual talents.

Dick used my talents on overseas missions—the flesh presser, the smiler. You go out, you eat the food, you talk to people, learn as much of the language as you can. You've got to relate to the people. Can you see a picture forming here? Cultivation of resources. Be aware of your surroundings. Teach the people new ideas, but be open yourself. Absorb their cultural knowledge. Don't look down your nose at them. Nobody likes being treated like that, and you'll never get anywhere if you act like that.

There wasn't a place I couldn't go in Egypt, Jordan, Pakistan, Morocco. We could fit in—not "I" but "we." But there always has to be that person who fits in a little bit quicker than the others, who becomes that impromptu leader. That was my capability. Dick recognized it, and capitalized on it.

• • •

We stayed in Washington, did OpNav 06-Delta and Red Cell, and that's the last time I was with them—'84 to '87. Dick was being pulled out of Red Cell because of the political bureaucratic bullshit. If you've read Book Number One, you saw some of the problems we were having. And yes, our charter was to do these exercises, but we were also a black bag charter. That's in print now, so nothing's compromised. But he was willing to ensure that we had what we needed to accomplish a mission someplace.

Of course, while we're doing the real-world missions, we're also doing a lot of those training exercises, working on security at the bases. That was interesting.

Complacency will kill you every time. There was an attitude of, "Oh well, it's just an inspection." And we weren't there to inspect anybody. We were there to test security facilities, security conditions. We'd walk around the base into the exchange, in and out of all kinds of buildings, secure areas, and we were almost never challenged. That's the God's honest truth.

One of our first exercises was down at Norfolk, on

the Naval Station and over at CINCLANFLT headquarters. Dick had some ID cards made up, all signed
for with his picture on them and his rank and rate. I
used one of the ID cards one day, drove up, showed
them Dick Marcinko's ID card, and I don't even look
like Dick. What happens is that these guards on the
gates see a pay grade on an ID card, and whew, that
snaps them up and they wave you on through.

So I drove all the way through to NAS. I even had a
frogman sticker on the back of the car. I'd put it there
on purpose, just to see if it would wake them up. And
it never stopped the normal routine flow of traffic. I
drove around NAS snapping pictures of the airplanes,
the helicopters, the airplane hangars. No attempt to
conceal my camera, no attempt to hide what I was
doing.

When we told the people at the base about it, they
said, "No, that can't happen. We didn't see anyone
out there. You people couldn't have been on that airfield."

"Well, let's watch the tape."

And there I am, snapping pictures of the airplane
hangar.

Now it's got their eyes open a little bit. They started
paying attention. But it was still very easy for us, in a
nonchalant manner, dressed in civilian clothes, to walk
about the base and go into buildings without even
being challenged.

One of the tasks I had was to go over to the communications center and simulate blowing the doors
down. So I took an artillery simulator and walked

right over to the com state, no problems. This is at night, in a well-lit parking lot, and I lit off that artillery simulator.

Well, when that goddamn thing went off, everybody knew *something* went off. I just walked away. Went to the turnstile gate. There was an Army major who was coming in the other side of the gate, and I know damn well he heard the noise. He said, "Are you lost?"

I said, "Yeah, I'm trying to get over to the O-Club."

"Oh, you go over here, and take a right."

This is *after* there'd been a huge explosion. Police cars are starting to show up all over the place. So there's sirens, all this noise, I'm wearing civilian clothes, carrying a backpack. And he just gives me directions.

I walked right out, over to the O-Club. I thought, "Let me see if I can pull something stupid here." I stopped a couple with their kid coming out of the O-Club. I asked them, "How can I get to Pizza Hut from here?"

They said, "Oh, come on, we'll give you a ride."

This is day three or four into the exercises, and these people are still doing this.

I get into the car, and before we got to the gate, I pulled out my radio. The little girl in the back with me says, "What's that?" The mother turns around, all panicked, and says, "What? What do you have?"

I said, "This is just a two-way radio. This is my badge and my ID card, this is who I am."

Her husband just melted in the driver's seat—"Oh, Jesus, am I in trouble now?"

I said, "Nah, but you better get me out the gate."

So I just sat in the back, and we were waved through the gate. There were two base police vehicles there. I can distinctly remember four base cops, but they're not checking anybody going out. So they drove me over to the Pizza Hut and I went on my merry way from there.

Everyone at the base was still thinking, "This is all just silly games." Or they just didn't care. Or they didn't know. Complacency.

And people are apprehensive about challenging people. One of the hardest things to overcome in teaching people security was to make them appreciate that it's okay to stop somebody and say, "Do you belong here? May I see some identification?"

It's just asking for ID. And if someone doesn't have proper ID, do you have a couple of people there to restrain that person from going any farther until you can contact the base police. There are too many places we went where they wouldn't do it. Even after we'd been there a week, they were still apprehensive about challenging people.

After our exercises were done, on just about all the bases, we'd tell them, "We're going to stick around for two more days, but there will be no more exercises." We'd sit around in the gate entry, the ship's quarterdeck, an airplane hangar, something like this, just watch people walking in and out. They're *still* apprehensive about challenging. I don't know what it is.

• • •

Steve Hartman and I had another project one night—if you want to call it night, it was two o'clock in the goddamn morning—where we left our hotel out there in town, in Sasebo, Japan. We've both got wet suits on, carrying a backpack, and I've got a floater bag. Got this picture? We walked down the street, by the gate to the base, over the bridge, and into the water. And nobody gave us a second look.

We swam that *beautiful* river, and we were so good that we didn't even scare the birds that were sitting on the rocks. We got up the mud embankment near the base. We'd told them on our survey, "There is a big, big hole under your fence here."

"Well, we're doing some construction there."

Dick told them, "That place could be a target. Your firehouse is right across the street." They never made any attempt at putting anybody near that hole.

Steve and I got in there and pulled our sneak-and-peek and I went across the street to the firehouse and planted the bomb, which was three simulated sticks of dynamite with a timer and a big flashbulb.

Next to the hole in the fence was a barracks with some Seabees in it, playing cards. Came back, and I saw one of the Seabees walk over to the window. I just lay down in the gutter. Waited, then I got up and peeked in the window. They're all playing cards, nobody's paying attention.

Steve and I lay in that mud for another two and a half hours until that thing went off. That whole time, in this well-lighted area, no one saw anything on the front of the fire truck, no one saw me, no one saw Steve.

After that thing went off, they wanted to know if we could reconstruct exactly what we did. So Steve and I walked them through it, a step at a time. "This is how we got in here, this is where we went, this is what I did." Pretty soon, they started posting people at that construction site, and nobody was getting through that hole.

•   •   •

One of the big problems that we had was convincing people that we're not there to hurt them, we're there to help. Some of the base COs just didn't like us being there. It took a lot of Dick's verbal persuasion to get that across to them. "This is not an inspection, you people have to understand that. It's an exercise. It's supposed to help you."

The amazing part is that some of the troops really *want* to be involved, even though the hierarchy tells them this is bullshit. "They're shutting our base down, they're making life miserable for us, they're making us look bad." But we *weren't* there to make them look bad, and some people got it.

One of the most cooperative groups we worked with was in Point Mugu, the security police there, a bunch of sailors. Captain Gordon Nakagawa and Lieutenant Bob Laser *wanted* their people tested, worked, beaten down and brought back up. And the kids were all for it. These were part-time, quick-response-team people. Anything we showed them, they absorbed like a sponge. The base admiral was an asshole, but we worked it anyway.

We said, "One of your weak spots is your response vehicles."

"What do you mean?"

"You got step vans out there, nobody's watching them. You got no motion detectors, no hidden cameras, no alarms, no nothing."

"Oh. Is that a problem?"

"Yes. That's a target. The next target is the airfield. You've got too much leeway, open here and open there, to where people can get in."

"Ah, but we got motion sensors there."

We told them, we can beat your motion sensors. And we showed them how. They absorbed this stuff. They were happy. Every time we'd go through an exercise, they'd say, "Goddamn it, another lesson learned."

•   •   •

Dick was always supportive of what we wanted to do. We'd come up with a game plan to change a scenario that had already been set—the guys at the base weren't playing by the rules. He's sitting right there, listening and writing it up. He's got a brain like a computer, it works so fast, and he'd say, "That's a good idea. Look at this option, this option, this option." So we'd rehearse it and say, "Hey, we can make this work." There were a lot of impromptu things that we did, because they kept wanting to change the goddamn rules, so we responded.

Dick also participated in some of the exercises to make sure we weren't tweaking the wrong things. There were times when that guy went with two hours' sleep. Sometimes we went two or three days when we were running ops twenty-four hours a day. He would monitor them, and it was his responsibility to defend them—"This is how they were done, this is where your weak spots are." Dick is a very, very articulate individual. In his own inimitable way, he can get his point across. But there were people who just continued to take it as an insult. When he had to, Dick stepped on a lot of toes. Well, that's too bad. The stupid bastards shouldn't have put their feet under his size twelve shoes.

But no matter how bad it was at a base, they almost always started to coalesce, at some point. We never left anyplace with bitter feelings, even though they always seemed to view us as big hairy monsters coming in to destroy their base. I remember something one of the base COs told us at one of the meetings. He was a good person who was willing to go along with things. He said, "You know, I come onto the base and I look at it and I think, 'What a nice place to be.' You fucking people come on board and say, 'What can I destroy?' "

And you know, he's right.

•   •   •

All the problems I've had with diving, I still love it. I really, really enjoyed the underwater work. It was very demanding, and it required you to concentrate. After that facial fracture, I was told, "You'll never dive again." I just said, "Well, watch my fucking lips and understand me." I pushed myself through it and I did it again. And the shooting—I used to throw myself into the shooting requirements, throw myself into honing those shooting skills. And it paid off a number of times.

I hated jumping out of a perfectly good goddamn airplane. But it was a requirement. I didn't have to like it, I just had to do it. So I did it. After a while, I'd just numb myself out to it. "Okay—going out again." And I went.

To motivate yourself, to overcome those things, you've got to eliminate negative thoughts. That insidious negativism that'll sneak in and bite you in the ass every time. You draw on your confidence, the experience of others, and you face that fear head-on. You make it work to your advantage. You're forceful. You start getting doubts, you start listening to that negativity, you've just defeated yourself.

• • •

I've had some good COs, don't get me wrong. But Dick was not only a leader, he was a teacher. He was a confidant. He was there to change your underwear if you shit your pants and fell asleep. People throw rocks at this guy—well, a number of us will stand there and take those rocks. Because he cared for his people. And there was a sense of, "Goddamn it, if the Old Man's doing it, I guess we can do it, too." He would lead you into it. And he would help you with it.

People looked at a lot of us like dirtbags. Troublemakers. But Dick looked a lot deeper than that. "Why is this little shithead getting into trouble? Why is *this* happening? Why is *that* happening?" And Dick would take on what other people considered dirtbags. Every one of us turned out to be star performers. He saw something, and he'd bring it out in you.

But he'd cut his losses, too. That's something I learned from him and used after I went on to become command master chief. You can give someone the tools. But if they don't put those tools to use, you hold them accountable and you cut your losses. And he was not afraid to do that.

• • •

From 1987 to 1990, I was the first command master chief at Naval Medical Research and Development Command. I put a lot of those leadership skills I'd learned from Dick to use, gave a whole new meaning to the word *leadership* at the senior enlisted level. I had eleven subordinate labs around the world, over four hundred enlisted personnel. I got enlisted recognition programs going, made goddamn sure they worked. I had a few can't-cunt COs who had to be told, "You're not doing it."

I had, fortunately, an XO at headquarters who cared also. He said, "Master Chief, can these programs work?"

"Captain, these goddamn programs will work if someone will kick the other COs in the ass. I've already kicked them in the shins, but someone with a little more horsepower has got to go a little higher."

So we made these programs work. You have to make the enlisted people part of what you're doing. That's something all of us learned from Dick. Draw in everyone from the lowest E-1 to the most senior E-9 and make them part of it. Listen to their input.

I had to do a lot of the security inspections and investigations, if you will, at the various labs. I put another twist on the word *security*. Actually, I brought it on board. These people had a security manual, and they ignored it. I said, "First thing, read the god-damned book. If you have questions, my telephone is available twenty-four hours a day, at work and at home." That's where we started.

Then I go out and enhance the physical security aspects and the people security aspects, particularly at the overseas labs. You've got these people—"I'm here as a researcher, a fucking rocket scientist, I can't see the forest for the trees." I told them, "You have to open your eyes."

From there, I went over to Newport, wound up being a department head—the only enlisted department head in the command, as well as the security officer. So I was able to put all that good stuff to use again, in a new setting.

• • •

I retired in 1992. Since then, I've been doing a lot of shooting, a lot of hunting, and a lot of fishing. Finally getting the time to play with my own toys. My wife retired the first of June, so I've actually got my wife back.

Since I left the Teams, I miss the closeness. Real closeness. I think the civilian community doesn't understand that. Even though some of us still maintain contact as a matter of routine, I know we'll probably not have that unique opportunity again. The times you were sent overseas—to Germany, to France, to Israel— for crosstraining, or out on missions where you're in each other's seabag twenty-four hours a day. You have to learn to be close. You set your personal prejudices aside, for the sake of the mission.

• • •

Some kind of teamwork training is needed, particularly at the corporate level. Too many in their ivory tower of power just don't appreciate what it's like to be in the trenches. Building a team, and the team-building concept—you'd be surprised how many corporate-level individuals have never been down on the work floor. All they know is that there are worker bees down there helping them make their seven-digit salaries per annum, with their stock options, their golden umbrella, their golden handshake at retirement. They don't know what he or she down there on the goddamn floor is doing.

If they would get down there and be visible—which is something Dick taught us, always—that would go a long way toward making some of these big corporations more viable. The people wearing the $2,000 Armani suits don't listen to the guy with the broom in his hands. And that guy, or that lady, might have some ideas to make that corporation more functional.

That's a skill I brought with me to command master chief. I listened to every enlisted sailor. I listened to some of the officers, too. Didn't listen to too goddamn many of them, because they didn't know what the hell they were talking about. They couldn't get their faces away from their microscopes and their petri dishes. But *listen* to what those sailors have to say. Listen to what those workers have to say. That's how you start building a team.

• • •

Terrorism seems to be our greatest problem scenario, internally and externally. The Special Warfare community is going to have a positive role in that. That's what they *should* have a role in. Because of the Posse Comitatus, we're not allowed to be actively participatory in these things. Externally, alliances have been formed with other nations, of course. The crosstraining that goes on, the personnel exchange programs—there is a large community of people in the overall Special Operations/Special Warfare community that are going to have an active role and will always have an active role. Hopefully the bureaucracy will recognize the need and continue to support the goals of the mission and allow these people to perform, and not chastise or hinder anyone's advancement because they chose this Special Warfare community.

The top-heaviness they've got now makes it very difficult to see a picture, and makes it even more difficult to get something off the ground and on the road. You've got some people out there who are just too goddamn interested in their own advancement. They've bureaucratized it. Every goddamn pencil has got to have a piece of paper justifying the pencil—every bullet, every this, every that—and then they start putting squashes on training scenarios. You start restricting people's training operations and training capabilities, and they start getting a little stale, they start getting demoralized, and they start getting very goddamn angry. Then the infighting starts. "Why are we here? What are we doing? You just spent a quarter of a mil-

lion dollars training my dumb ass—are you going to
let me put any of this to use?"

I believe the Teams ought to have a more broadened
role in all theaters of operation. And instead
of someone spending an entire career on the East
Coast, move them back and forth every six or eight
years, so all Team members can interface with those in
both parts of the world and have an idea about what's
going on there. It'll always be two separate areas of
responsibility, but at least let those who've been dealing with this side of the world get exposed to the other
side, so you do have a rounded Spec Warfare community.

Their role in the future I see as what it is now—intelligence gathering, counterintelligence, counterterrorism, antiterrorism. We must not ever forget the teaching aspect. I see them as teachers. There are a lot of
countries emerging out there that are looking for direction in a lot of areas. One of them is, "What do I do for
a military unit?" Now you have the people on hand to
go over and train these people. Train these people the
right way. The Teams can be used in that manner, and
they should be.

Debriefing

So there you go—words of wisdom from the Real Team, ten true Warriors. Aren't they great? But you can't have 'em, they're mine. You've got to go out there and build your own Real Team. Of course you can do it. Review the nine guidelines at the start of the book. Think about what each man said affected him, motivated him, made a big difference in his performance. What did each man take with him when he left the Teams?

Need a refresher on the nine guidelines? Here they are:

- It's the mission, stupid. Be clear and precise in defining your goals and objectives.

- Get your numbers straight. When it comes to time and money, ask for what you want, but know what you really *need*.

- Cover all the positions. Determine what skills your operators will need and make sure you don't leave any holes. Surround yourself with talent.

- Keep your hands off. Trust your people to do their jobs. Micromanaging leads to macrofuck-ups.

- Know your men—they're not machines. Know their strengths and weaknesses. Know what's going on "behind the scenes" that might affect their work.

- Welcome mistakes. Capitalize on this opportunity to improve the team's performance.

- Shut up and listen. Encourage your men to contribute to problem solving. They'll support what they help create. Clear communication always needs two-way signal flow.

- Share the wealth. Reward your team when they've done well. Money's great, but be creative.

- Eat the pain. Take on your responsibilities as the team leader. Remember, loyalty is a two-way street.

The Ongoing Effort

Since I'm not willing to share my Team with you, the least I can do is help you find and develop your own team of warriors in your own warriorlike image.

Again, I'm borrowing from *Enlightened Leadership* for these five ways to keep yourself flowing and going in a positive direction.

1. Celebrate your team's small successes.

2. Take a good hard look at what you're doing to create those successes.

3. Focus and refocus on your specific objectives.

4. Help everyone—your team members, everyone else in the organization, your customers, your shareholders—understand the overall benefits of achieving your objectives.

5. Keep searching for ways to improve your progress toward your objectives.

Maybe you've gotten to this point in the book, and you're feeling like your situation is too complicated, too hard for you to deal with on your own. Well, remember I said I was putting together a way to teach leadership and team-building skills effectively? Here's the intel on that effort.

At the CrossRoads

CrossRoads Training and Development Center will combine the focus and exhilaration you can get only through hard physical effort with practical, useful information. These two aspects of leadership training will work in tandem to make a real difference in the abilities and skills of our clients. And these skills will be imparted by real Warriors, true leaders—former SEALs and former U.S. Marines.

CrossRoads will offer programs tailored and customized to our clients' needs. You can choose from leadership seminars, corporate team-building exercises, business war-gaming, youth and adolescent development programs, seminars specifically tailored for women, and tactical courses for all levels of law enforcement. If you and your family want to spend a long weekend there, you can. If you and your management team need to learn how to pull together, bring 'em all down to CrossRoads.

One Last Word

I want to leave you with a little wisdom from one of our country's greatest Warriors, General Patton. In June 1944, he gave a speech to the American troops in England. He had a lot of brilliant things to say about training and about overcoming fear, but the thing that struck me most was the following description he gave of one specific soldier.

"One of the bravest men I ever saw was a fellow on top of a telegraph pole in the midst of a furious firefight in Tunisia. I stopped and asked what the hell he was doing up there at a time like that. He answered, 'Fixing the wire, sir.' I asked, 'Isn't that a little unhealthy right about now?' He answered, 'Yes, sir, but the goddamned wire has to be fixed.' I asked, 'Don't those planes strafing the road bother you?' And he answered, 'No, sir, but you sure as hell do!'

"Now, there was a real man. A real soldier. There was a man who devoted all he had to his duty, no matter how seemingly insignificant his duty might appear at the time, no matter how great the odds."

Amen to that.

ADD THESE

ROGUE WARRIOR®

BOOKS FROM RICHARD MARCINKO, AND JOHN WEISMAN TO YOUR COLLECTION

Echo Platoon

Option Delta

Seal Force Alpha

Designation Gold

Task Force Blue

Green Team

Red Cell

Rogue Warrior

AND FROM RICHARD MARCINKO

Leadership Secrets of the Rogue Warrior

The Rogue Warrior's Strategy for Success

Visit www.SimonSays.com/rogue

POCKET BOOKS
A VIACOM COMPANY

Visit the

ROGUE WARRIOR®

at

www.SimonSays.com/rogue

where you can read excerpts
from his books, find a listing
of future titles, and learn more
about the Rogue Warrior®
and his mission!

POCKET BOOKS

Not sure what to read next?

Visit Pocket Books online at

www.SimonSays.com

Reading suggestions for
you and your reading group

New release news

Author appearances

Online chats with your favorite writers

Special offers

And much, much more!

POCKET BOOKS
A Division of Simon & Schuster
A VIACOM COMPANY

**POCKET
STAR BOOKS**
A Division of Simon & Schuster
A VIACOM COMPANY

10421